LEGEND
OF THE
CHEROKEE
MAPS

RAY APPLETON

authorHOUSE®

AuthorHouse™
1663 Liberty Drive
Bloomington, IN 47403
www.authorhouse.com
Phone: 833-262-8899

Published by AuthorHouse 03/01/2021

ISBN: 978-1-6655-1812-3 (sc)
ISBN: 978-1-6655-1811-6 (e)

Library of Congress Control Number: 2021904061

INTRODUCTION

The year is 1859. Rumors of secession and possible war over slavery are the main topics of all conversation. Most everyone knows that the state of South Carolina is leading the secessionist movement in Congress. Union Army Intelligence agents have come up with a plan to map all of the hidden trails and possible routes through the lower Appalachians, especially the Great Smoky Mountain range, using Cherokee Indian guides to help their surveyors. They feel that with this knowledge, they would be able to move men and supplies through this region undetected. All the Army has to do is talk the Cherokee into it.

CHAPTER 1

KNOXVILLE, TN

T HE MORNING STARTED out like so many mornings here recently. After my break-up with Karen, I spend too many nights out hitting the clubs trying to find someone to fill the gap left in my soul by her leaving. So, I wake up feeling like this, somewhere just south of hangover hell. Fortunately, my job has become so routine, it very seldom requires my full attention. If there is going to be anything serious to apply myself to, I usually have a few days notice and will forego my nightly binges.

I finished my morning ritual of shower, shave, coffee, and Visine, then headed out for my office. Normally, traffic isn't too bad here in Knoxville, unless some over-zealous trucker fails to take the by-pass and doesn't make one of the sharp curves through town. But today was uneventful and I arrived at the offices of Fenton, Bruce, and Hawkes pretty much on time. We aren't the biggest law firm in eastern Tennessee, but between our office here and the one in Atlanta, we boast 12 full partners, 30 junior partners, and who knows how many associates, para-legals and staff. We all strive diligently on a daily basis to make sure that the industrial, commercial, and real-estate rights of our clients are well defended. Not criminal law like I had wanted in college, but a boring, mundane practice that pays well. It probably also helps that my last name is Hawkes, and after 7 years now, I am a junior partner following in my father's footsteps. Well, sort of.

One of our largest clients is the Eastern Band of the Cherokee Indians. A very lucrative account, whose expansions and additions to the casino are always requiring some form of legal representation. Being half Cherokee on my father's side, and having family on the tribal council, is a big plus also. That's why I wasn't in the least surprised when a call came in from my crazy cousin Red Legs. He was his usual boisterous self, threatening me with a slow, torture filled death if I didn't make it down to see him in the near future. According to him, all the big deer in the Great Smoky Mountains had somehow wandered onto reservation land, or just south of highway 74 and were just waiting for me to come hunt them down. He swore by all the Gods that he had seen so many big bucks that we could just sit on the cabin porch and wait for a 16 point to just walk up and offer itself to us! He also said something about if I didn't come this year, he was going to vote in council to discontinue using my services, since the only time I showed up was just for funerals. He was right of course, and I did need to visit my grandfather who was getting on in years. He had taught me how to hunt, fish, track, and live off of the land every summer for 15 years. After talking with Red, I felt better and decided it was time to go see them all. I'd been doing nothing but chasing my tail, or any tail, since Karen left and could use a break from the routine bachelor life. I looked at my calendar and didn't see anything pressing, at least nothing that I couldn't assign to an associate. And with the EBCI being one of our largest clients, I could probably find someway to get paid for it!

"Lucy!" I called to the secretary that was one of my most valuable assets. She is as smart as they come and a tireless worker as well as a big fan of mine. Always ready to protect me from the evils of corporate law. Screening my calls and ever vigilant watching for the arrival of Mr. Floyd Cameron Hawkes the first, letting me know well in advance when His Majesty was coming. Being Floyd Cameron Hawkes the second had earned me the title of "Deuce", as I did not feel like a Floyd, and didn't respond well to Junior either. Everyone called my father Cameron, or Cam, so that was out. So it was my grandfather who stuck the moniker Deuce on me at about 6 years old. Cameron didn't like it much, but after awhile, I wouldn't answer to anything else.

"Yeah, hon?" Lucy asked as she walked in.

"I think I'm going to the reservation for a few days. I need you to…no, wait, I think I'll go for 2 weeks. How are things looking on the Hollister deal? Anything that Micheal or Kevin can't take care of?" I asked her. She flipped open her day planner that I have honestly never seen her without. Rumor has it she sleeps with it.

"Nothing jumps right out, Deuce, but are you going to clear it with you know who?"

"Nope! Look, if I don't get out of here for awhile, I'm going to self-destruct. Anyway, if he has a problem with it, he can call and leave a message at Grandfather's lodge or the casino. Other than that 2 day trip to Pensacola Beach last summer, I haven't taken any of my vacation time."

I gave her my best 'devil-may-care' smile and began dictating memos for her to give to my associates. When we finished, I kissed her on the cheek and headed for the elevator, calling Red Legs as I walked.

"Hey cuz! Get the guns and bows ready. You have aroused the heathen in me and I am ready to shoot something!" I told him when he answered.

"Alright bro! Don't bring anything but clothes and a toothbrush. I got ya covered. Should I line up some company for you? I told all the single girls about my big city cousin lawyer, and you might get lucky!"

"No thanks Red. I just want to go hunting, do some hiking and camping, visit with Grandfather and what not. Don't need the casino package or any company. Been doing enough of that since Karen left. Just let me borrow that 30.06 I got you for Christmas a few years back."

"No problem, cousin. How long are you staying for? I really do have a couple of issues to discuss with you about some tribal purchases for the museum."

"Oh, at least a week, maybe 2. I want to go down below the ridge, you know, where we used to sneak off to when we were kids. Hunt the west ridge of the Plott Balsams, and over around Wilmot and Alarka. Man, there are places back in there that no one even knows about."

"Okay, bro. I can go with you for a few days at least. We can hunt down where the old lodge used to be. I snuck down there and fixed up one of the old cabins. It ain't no Hilton, but the stove works and the roof don't leak. So, see ya tonight."

The drive down is fourlane all the way now. With Sevierville, Gatlinburg, and Harrah's Casino all becoming such big tourist attractions, it made the drive a practice in patience. But, I was out to relax and chill anyway, so I just eased along like any other tourist. I still made it in good time, letting the Beamer run when it could, hugging the curves and winding roads like she was meant to. Red met me at the casino and we drove over to see my grandfather. I couldn't believe that he had not changed perceptibly in 5 years. He still had the long thick white hair and look of eternal wisdom, along with that little smile that made you wonder what it was that he knew and you didn't. He greeted me like it was yesterday that I had left, never once mentioning the fact that it had been years. I informed him that I was staying for at least 2 weeks. He smiled and said that would be wonderful if I did. Then he leaned back, yawned, and was snoring again in seconds.

Red came in a few minutes later and had a frown on his face. I could tell something was wrong when he flopped down in the chair.

"What's the matter, cuz?" I asked. He looked at me with his huge brown eyes and shook his head.

"It seems there is something I must take care of in Raliegh. I knew this was coming up, but I had hoped it would wait until after we went hunting. I have to leave tomorrow, but I'll be back in 3 or 4 days."

"Is there anything you need me for, or the firm?" I asked.

"No, nothing like that. I just have to review some purchases being made for the casino. Part of the new décor we are working on with Harrah's. Some of the elders want them changed. Too gaudy, is their word. But, I'll only be gone a few days at most. Why don't you hang out at the casino, I'll comp you, then we'll go when I get back?"

"That's alright, Red. You go do what you gotta do, and Im going camping, maybe fish a bit. When you get back, come to the cabin, and if I'm not there, I'll have a map drawn showing you where I'm at."

"Hell, city boy, you sure you won't get lost or hurt down there? I mean, its been what? 5 years since you have been down here? You still got your Indian ways about ya?"

"Yeah, I think I can still tell north from south, and know which end of the horse kicks. I haven't forgotten a damn thing you and Grandfather drilled into me for all those years!"

"Okay, okay, man, I know you can take care of yourself. Come on, let's go over to the stables and I'll pick you out a couple of good horses that ride smooth and don't spook easy. I'll have one of the guy's hook-up the trailer to my jeep. Stop by and see Callie at the kitchen and she'll put a grub sack together for you. Then I guess I'll fly to Raleigh by myself. No one wants to fly with me in our little Cessna, the Red Legs Express!"

CHAPTER 2

THE DEER

AFTER A SLOW drive of about 2 hours, the rugged road turned into a trail too narrow for the jeep and trailer. I parked and unloaded the horses from the trailer. I saddled the paint and loaded my supplies on the roan. I had brought her in case I did shoot a deer and had to pack it out.

The piebald paint that Red had chosen for me was as sure-footed as a mountain goat and as easy natured as any horse can be. Which was a good thing, because no matter what I'd told Red, it didn't take much to realize how long it had been since I'd spent a day in the saddle. By the time I had ridden over the first pass, known as Angel's Rest, I already had the beginnings of a good set of saddle sores. A slow gentle ride was what I needed. But Red was right about the deer population. There were plenty of big bucks throughout this area. I had spotted at least 10 that would go 8 to 12 points, but for some reason, I wasn't up to shooting one yet. I found myself just riding along, enjoying the scenery and admiring the beauty of nature at work. Hadn't seen any bears yet, but did see plenty of spoor and signs that they were around. I would leave it up to the horses to let me know when one was near.

About an hour or so later, I came to the cabins. All but one was in total shambles, but the one wasn't too bad. Red had fixed it up enough that it would keep the bears out and keep you dry. After an easy dinner of smoked sausage and beans, I stoked the fire up and lay down on the cot, thinking that maybe I should build a cabin down here. Come down on weekends, work on it with Red. Get away from the bars and nightlife, and who knows, maybe scout around for the future Mrs. Hawkes. With these thoughts on my mind, I drifted off to sleep.

I woke up to the sounds of nature, a cacophony of birds and insects letting the world know that this was their playground. No hangover, no rushing around to get ready for another mundane, boring day at work in the jungle of corporate law. I loaded up enough food for a couple of days and left Red a note telling him where I was heading. Just following the stream towards Alarka Mountain. The horses and I were just easing our way through the valley. The panoramic background and early chill had put me into a state of meditation and awe, bringing back once again the longing for a simpler life. As I rested under a small bluff, I gazed into the deeper shadows bordering a granite cliff face. I found myself looking between 2 huge cliffs and into a valley that I don't remember ever having discussed with Red or Grandfather. The thick stand of trees and brush had made the perfect camouflage, and I probably would have never seen it had the sun not been shining just right to reflect off of the granite face. I turned the horse down the hill towards the valley and cliffs, and among the thick grove of trees stood a sight to behold! A majestic buck had appeared, the likes of which are very seldom seen! He stood nearly as tall as my horse, and at first I wondered what an elk was doing in North Carolina? I eased off of the horse, slipping my rifle from the scabbard as I landed. The moccasins I had on made not a sound as I began to ease into a firing position among the dead fall. It was a good 75 yard shot. I balanced the rifle on a tree branch for support and began sighting in my scope. Everything was perfect, breeze blowing uphill, and as I trained my sights on him, he turned, staring straight at me! As if daring me to shoot one so regal in demeanor. I just froze, staring back at him, hypnotized by his strength and beauty! I guess it was a clear-cut case of buck fever! But now, I believe it was all for a reason.

As we stared at each other, he made a snorting noise that I heard all the way up the hill. He coiled like a spring, then leapt completely over the bush in front of him and was gone!

I slung the rifle into the scabbard, mounted my horse and headed for the copse of trees that he had disappeared into. I now swapped my rifle for the Canon camera I had brought, determined to get a photo of this magnificent animal. Time to see if my childhood training would come back, to see if I could still track a deer.

Once I reached the brush where he had been grazing, I tied the horses to a tree and began a slow, methodical study of the ground until I found where he had landed. An astonishing 20 feet or better from takeoff! His deep tracks indicated that he was pretty heavy. At a guess, I'd say 350-400 pounds, huge for a whitetail in these parts. I tracked him into another stand of birch and as I stared at him, he raised his head affording me the perfect picture. I snapped off several before he turned to his right and seemed to just disappear into a solid granite wall! Just gone! As I approached the massive rock face, there seemed to be a darker area at the base of the cliff. I pushed my way through the brush, only to find a cave opening made by 2 sheer rock walls leaning against each other. The opening was about 10 feet tall at the apex, and about 10 feet wide also. I stared into it and as my eyes adjusted, began to realize that there was light shining through the cave. I went back to my horse and made sure I had snake shot in my pistol, grabbed a flashlight, flash for the camera and a bottle of water. Now equipped, I entered the cave.

Admittedly, I felt some trepidation upon entering the cave. I am a long way from anywhere, so if anything went wrong…well, I'm up shit creek, as they say. I was watching my feet carefully, because it seemed to me that if I were a rattler, hell yeah I'd live in here!

The cave went back some 30 feet or so and began to curve to the left. As I rounded the curve, I found myself staring at a lush paradise enclosed in a box canyon! The kind you only read about in some old Louis L'Amour novel. At the edge of a clearing, the majestic stag stood staring at me, as if daring me to enter his domain. I looked behind me and the entrance was no longer visible. It was a perfect blind spot. I thought there was a good chance that no man had ever been in here before! I began to scan the tops of the granite walls and could see huge old oak trees with limbs hanging down for dozens of feet from the top of the ridge. The trees made a complete canopy overhead, and no one could ride through the thick brush up there, or even think about looking down. I started to walk toward the deer, slowly bringing my camera up. I could tell by all of the flattened grass that this had been his refuge for years. It looked as if maybe 10 –20 deer had bedded down here recently. All part of his harem and offspring, no doubt. As I began to take more pictures, it seemed to me as if we had rehearsed this moment, as he gradually turned toward me, seeming to pose for the shot. He seemed to know that he was THE DEER, the one so many had hunted for years and never but glimpsed occasionally. He snorted at the mere mortal I am and began to trot toward the back of the canyon, leaving me only his posterior to view as he disappeared again into the brush.

My battery pack now exhausted, I returned to the cave and exited to my horse. I was hoping to persuade the critter into walking through the cave with me, even though horses are notoriously skittish in tight confines. But, thanks to Red's keen choice of horseflesh, they both let me quietly walk them through the cave and in to the box canyon. I mounted the paint and tied the roan to a tree, then began a slow exploration of the westside of the canyon walls, planning on making a full circuit to see how big the canyon was, to see if there were any other exits. The possibility of a bear or cougar being in here wasn't very likely or the stag wouldn't have been so relaxed. But the idea of stumbling across the stag and startling him was just as worrisome. A creature of that size and weight could do some serious damage with that massive set of horns!

Not more than 50 feet from the cave, I paused to scan my back tracks and noticed how different the scenery was. How quickly it had changed. The old growth trees were all centered in mass, while the outer trees near the edge of the wall were smaller, younger. The center was home to trees over a hundred feet tall, and several hundred years old. The outer trees were also huge, but didn't seem to be as ancient. Maybe only 100-150 years old. I'm no botanist, and all of this was just a guess due to the surrounding forest, but as I slowly rode and studied the natural fault lines of the granite, it suddenly became clear what I was looking at. It was an ancient sinkhole of enormous proportions. Sometime in the far past, the center of this old mountain had fallen in. The ancient trees in the center had survived, while new life sprang up all around them! Awesome, just freaking awesome, I thought. I took out my binoculars and scanned as far as I could up the walls. They were at least 200 feet straight up. The trees growing along the edges up top leaned over creating the canopy that completely covered the edge of the canyon. As I brought my vision down the walls, a reflection in a nearby tree caught my eye. I refocused, and there it was again. Something shiny was reflecting what little sunlight managed to intrude here. I eased the mare forward, trying to keep the shiny spot in view. Several times I lost sight of it and had to backtrack until I could see it again. As I neared the cave entrance, I spotted it once more and was able to tell which tree it was coming from. It seemed to be something metallic causing the reflection. I was able to ride up to the object, and even on horseback, it was still a foot above my head. It appeared to be a knife tip protruding from the tree trunk.

CHAPTER 3

THE GRAVE

I SAT THERE STARING at the knife tip, then drew out my own knife and began to whittle away at the bark, wondering how in the hell a knife had gotten embedded in this old tree. As I uncovered more of the old blade, it was obvious now that I wasn't the first person to stumble across this hidden canyon. The old blade was deeply embedded and was a very large knife, not so much wide but very long. It was running east and west and as I traced the length of the blade, I was surprised to find a rusted hoop protruding from the other side of the tree, making it over 2 feet long. Sitting and staring at the long blade, it finally dawned on me that it wasn't a knife, but an old bayonet! Apparently, it had been lodged in this tree decades ago at ground level when the tree was very young. The tree had grown around it, causing it to bend and gradually curve with the tree. I moved the mare to the side of the tree so I could get a better angle with my hunting knife to try and dig the bayonet out without it breaking. As I removed more of the meat of the tree, I never thought to look up any further. Not until the mare moved and I had to regain my grip on the tree. Imagine my surprise when I discovered another bayonet tip just barely showing through about a foot above the first one! Only this one was running north and south, intersecting the first one in the middle, forming a perfect cross! It was then I realized that I might be standing on someone's grave! Horse and all! I began to back the mare slowly away from the tree. What little light penetrated back this far was fading fast, and my better senses were telling me to ease back to the cave and stay the night, continue this exploration in the broad daylight!

I unsaddled the paint and hobbled her just outside of the cave entrance. She would be a good alarm for anything else that might want to use this cave overnight. I cleared a spot for my bedroll and gathered some rocks for a fire pit, along with enough wood to last the night. After the fire was going and the coffee water was on, I settled back against my saddle and relaxed. I poured my first cup and leaned back, letting my eyes wander up and down the walls of the cave. I could tell by the stains and water marks which way the water ran when it rained. It seemed to go under the granite, washing out a spot 6-8 inches wide and about 6 inches deep alongside of the wall. As I stared at the wall, I began to notice a set of vertical marks uniform enough to know they weren't natural. I grabbed my canteen, wet my bandana and began washing away the dirt and grime. It soon became obvious that the marks were the vertical lines commonly used for the counting of days, like you would see in some prison movie where the inmate marks his time by scratching on the wall..llll… with a bar across them../…There were 2 sets of these, then..lll..So, I'm guessing 13 of something? Days? 13 days of what? Until what? I wet the bandanna again and grabbed my flashlight, then washed off a spot about 6 feet high by 10 feet wide. I began to examine the wall more closely. Other marks were starting to appear. I then had an idea. I always carried a bottle of baby powder to keep my feet dry when hiking. I dug it out and began to throw the powder against the damp wall. As I blew away the excess powder, other forms started to appear. One was an orb or circle with an arrow in it, pointing to the rear of the cave, or outside of the cave, or well, anywhere actually. The next carving was a box with a star in it. I got right up to wall, only inches away, and letters began to take shape. It took me another 10 minutes of close scrutiny to finally put the letters together to make a sentence.

'Sgt Burton Combs'. That part was pretty clear. The next letters weren't all that clear, but I thought it was an S…then a CS..and what was either an A or an M. Then 1859 was definitely clear. After that, it was just a mish-mash of letters where only a few words were legible, like …here…dying.. and..gold'. But the words in between were anybody's guess. I sat back and considered what little I knew so far: (1) there is a cross in a tree.(2) 1859 was 160 years ago, so it was a small tree then. (3) the markings on the wall were most likely made by someone laying down. (4) the grave is most likely that of someone named Sgt. Burton Combs, who lie here dying and scratched his last days on the wall. And (5) the word gold, which is enough to get anyone's blood pumping!

As my batteries started to dim, I gave up searching for more words or signs. I stoked the fire and began to wonder, who the hell was Sgt. Burton Combs, and if those letters say CSA, what was a Confederate sergeant doing back in here in 1859? The war hadn't even started yet!

The morning sun came shining through the cave entrance, and the mare was nosing around looking for me. I can't remember having slept so well in ages. Yeah, it was a little cool, but the heavy sleeping bag and the fire in the cave had kept me plenty warm all night. I stoked the fire back up and reheated last night's coffee. 2 cups of this stuff would fuel a double A dragster. With the coffee and a protein energy bar, I was ready to pick up where I had left off last night. I saddled the paint and led her through again with no problem, tying her off not far from the 'bayonet tree'. I took my little fold-up camp shovel and hunting knife and began to gingerly dig around at the base of the tree. I felt somewhat ghoulish when I thought about what I was doing, kind of like grave robbing. But it paid off pretty quick. After only a few minutes, I discovered several metal artifacts. The first was a brass button, then a few minutes later, an oval piece of metal about 4 inches long and 3 inches wide. Then after that, what I'm pretty sure was the barrel and cylinder of an old pistol. I began to wonder if Red knew anyone at the reservation that had a metal detector. I decided to leave the grave site alone until I could bring one back, then went back into the cave.

I sat down in front of the markings on the wall. Thirteen marks, a round orb, an arrow pointing to the other wall, maybe, and a box with a star in it. Following the natural watercourse along the basin of the cave, it coincided with the arrow. So, on hands and knees I began to crawl along the floor, searching under the lip that had been washed out by decades of rain. If he (Sgt Combs) had been lying down when he chiseled those marks, it would certainly account for why they were so low. I lay down and positioned myself so that I could reach up to the marks, then began digging against the wall as far as I assumed he could've reached.

And then my hand hit something round! I rolled over and started digging faster, then stared into the gap I had made. Staring back at me was the cylindrical end of what looked like a beer can! I laughed out loud and thought that maybe this cave wasn't as secluded as I had believed. Red would probably tell me of parties they had been having back here for years! I studied the can again, and figured what the hell, might as well dig it out and see how old of a can it is. I dug with just my hands at first, until it became obvious that it was longer than any damn beer can, much longer! Now I switched to my knife and camp shovel, and finished uncovering what seemed to be a metal tube about 2 feet long. It had been covered in something, but the something had rotted away long ago. There were bright yellow scratch marks where my knife had scraped it. I was finally able to extract it from the hole, and still had no clue as to what it was. It was sealed at both ends, and I had a feeling it was still watertight. If I opened it now, I could ruin whatever was inside. I shook it, but didn't hear anything rattle.

I gathered up the metal objects I had unearthed and led the mare back outside. It was time to go. My curiosity wasn't going to be satisfied here. I needed to get back to the reservation and contact someone about this, someone who knew much more than I about antiquities. And I knew just the person.

After leaving the canyon, I turned back to the east and tried to ride up to the top of the bluff, see if I could find the depression from above. The beauty and majesty of the granite outcrops and old growth trees were worth several pictures. After about an hour, I gave up on trying to locate the canyon from above. There was one valley that may have wound down behind it, but the thick brush and undergrowth made it obvious that there were no animal trails or paths leading into the canyon. It was as secluded as a deserted island.

On the ride to the cabin, I marked a few trees so that I could find my way back later. It was while I was carving an X on one tree, that I spotted what I think was the same deer. He was standing on a ridge above me with several other deer around him. He seemed to be staring straight at me, totally fearless. After a few seconds he made that snorting noise again, then he and his harem darted into the thicket. I felt a cold chill run down my spine as I rode off, thinking he was trying to warn me about something. I shrugged it off and began thinking about the brass tube and what might be in it. The word gold scratched on the wall made me wonder if there might be a treasure map inside. And where there was gold, there was usually trouble.

After I dropped the horses and trailer off at the stables, I headed for Grandfather's lodge. I was hoping that Red would be back by now so I could blow his mind with the pictures of the deer, canyon, and bayonets. And the brass tube. He was going to have to go back with me. This was turning into an adventure like something we would have made up as kids. Grandfather was gone and his housekeeper said Red had not returned yet, so I headed to the motel at the casino and checked in. After a couple of drinks and a shower, I downloaded the camera into the computer and went to the front desk to use their printer.

The pictures were even more astounding when printed on the high gloss paper. I took them and went back to the room, ordered supper, and called my dad. I explained to him what was going on, about the vacation, not the artifacts. I was actually asking him for permission, kind of. Seems he was all good with me taking some time off and visiting his father, even hinting that he wished he could be there, too. He is Cherokee, after all. I was just fixing to tell him about the brass tube and other stuff, but for some reason, I didn't. I just said that I had found some old buttons and a piece of an old pistol down by the cabins. Then I mentioned an old friend of his that I had met at one of the dozens of social parties the firm was always having. A professor of archaeology and anthropology at the University of Tennessee in Knoxville, one of Dad's alumni brothers.

Dad laughed out loud, "Mr. Andy Jack? Sure, sure, I'll text his number to you. He's a good guy. Done countless hours of work for us over the years, even for several other tribes in the south and east. Hell, sometimes he even got paid for it! You'll like him. Just remember, if you get put-off by his know-it-all attitude, or if he acts like he's so much smarter than you, it's no act. He is!"

Dad texted me the number to Andrew Jackson Hartshorne, or Andy Jack. I gave him a call and was delighted to catch him still at the university. We exchanged pleasantries after I explained who I was, and of course I had to fill him in on how Dad was doing and when the next party was scheduled. Then I explained to him my reason for calling. After describing the cylinder and brass pieces to him, I could tell by his voice he was getting excited.

"You haven't tried to open, have you?" he asked.

"No sir, it seems to still be watertight and I was afraid of damaging the contents." "Good, very good! We can use my grad students for the labor and open it in the antiquities vault under laboratory conditions, thereby assuring no damage to the contents. It sounds to me as if you have found an old cylindrical map or documents case, possibly dating back to the Civil War! In which case, we must use the utmost care in opening it, there being no telling what it might contain! And you say it is still sealed? Good God, young man! I would have you bring it now if I were not already requested elsewhere! But lets do have a look at it …say about 9:00 a.m. tomorrow? How does that suit you?"

"Yes sir, that will be fine by me. I can hardly wait!"

His enthusiasm was infectious. If I had to sit here and stare at the damn thing all night, I wasn't going to last without trying to open it. I headed down to the casino to play a little blackjack to keep my mind off of it. After I had lost just about what the free room would have cost me for the week, I headed up to bed. As I lay there, my last thoughts were… this is the place in some cheesy mystery novel where the bad guys show up and steal the treasure map.

I left about 7:00 a.m. the next morning and enjoyed an almost traffic free drive back to Knoxville. When I entered the museum I spotted Professor Hartshorne pacing the floor in front of a display case filled with dozens of Civil War artifacts, including several cylindrical cases similar to mine. He immediately headed my way with his hand stuck out, and as I stuck out mine, thinking we were going to shake, he bypassed my hand and went straight to the cylinder!

"I do believe you have something of a find here, my boy! If you'll look in the display case, you will see some similar to your, but with the leather still intact. Notice all of the stains on yours'? That was caused by the deterioration of several layers of waterproofing and dye on the leather before it rotted off. This one seems to have been buried for quite some time, eh? The wax seals are all gone externally, but it seems to be sealed internally; one can only hope that it is threaded and not just plugged and waxed! Hopefully everything is intact and legible! If you'd be so kind as to allow me to open it, we will take the utmost care in doing so, and you won't find a better dry-air vault in the tri-state area! And you know, we must

15

discuss where you found these items, and what price you'd like to have for the case...oops...so sorry, getting ahead of myself. Let's go open it first!"

"The very reason I called you, sir. I knew you would know what to do." I said to his back, as he was almost sprinting down the hall.

"Well, come on then, lets get to it!" he yelled back over his shoulder.

I stood outside of the glass enclosure and watched as 2 of the professor's grad students donned white coats, rubber gloves, linen gloves, and then placed surgical masks over their nose and mouth. They looked more like surgeons than any archeologist I had ever seen. After clamping the tube in place with a rubber coated vise, they began trying to open the tube by hand. Nope, wasn't going to happen that way! So they began using an assortment of small chisels and tools that to me looked awfully similar to a lock pick set. They sprayed some type of solvent on the ends and managed to clear all of the grime and debris away. It was impossible to tell which end, or if both ends were threaded. When one end actually started to turn, I found myself holding my breath as it came off! As the professor looked inside of the tube, a smile began to spread across his face. He gingerly extracted a rolled tube of paper.

"Mr Hawkes! We will now attempt to unroll these documents and place them between sheets of glass, then seal the edges. No rocket science here young man, just common sense! Shouldn't take much longer. An hour at the most."

After about 45 minutes, I realized that I had been pacing the floor, thinking this must be what an expectant father feels like. The professor came bouncing down the hall with his entourage of interns and grad students hustling to keep up.

"Mr. Hawkes, Mr. Hawkes! These documents are very well preserved!" he exclaimed. "We have begun to scan the pages with the digital camera, putting everything on the wall screen at 20 times magnification. Come see! Come see!"

It seemed that the 1st page was a set of orders to a Sgt. Burton L. Combs of the South Carolina Militia. The orders were from a Maj. Albert G. Blanchard asking him to help pick a team of 4 men for a clandestine operation. The only requirements were that they all had to be skilled woodsmen, and they must be Secessionist sympathizers. He and the men were then to proceed with the utmost haste to the Charleston residence of the Major, where they would then be given the mission target and goal.

The second page was a stock requisition for supplies and outfits for five men, and a list of the men and the ranks they were to be issued, as well as the monthly payment they were to receive from the South Carolina Militia. The list of men; Clancy Moore, Daniel Desmond, Christopher Olden, Dennis Cole, Sgt. Burton Combs.

The professor assigned a student to each of the names and sent them buzzing into cyberspace to see what they could find out about each man. The next document really got my attention. It was from a half-breed Cherokee from South Carolina stationed at Ft. Rend, Tennessee. It seems he had come across some information that the Union had made a deal with the Cherokee. They had recruited quite a number of the Indians to act as guides for the Union surveyors as they mapped the trails and passes through the Lower Appalachians and Great Smoky Mountains. These maps were to be delivered to a Union soldier, one Lt. Brandon O'Shea, in exchange for gold and land titles. The rendezvous was to be at an Indian hunting camp on the Tennessee River, not far from a settlement known as Almond, North Carolina. The meeting was set for September 1st, 1859.

It seems that the Sergeant's team and he were tasked with intercepting the Union couriers and taking possession of the gold. They were then to impersonate the Union soldiers and meet with the Cherokee and buy the maps, or take possession of them by any means possible. The ultimate goal was to return to Major Blanchard with the maps, but if this proved impossible, then they were to destroy the maps. If the maps fell into Union hands, the results could prove deadly in the near future, should South Carolina decide to secede from the Union.

CHAPTER 4

Lt. Brandon O'Shea- U.S. Army -Ft Rend, Tennessee

January, 1859

"**G**OOD MORNING MAJOR Jenkins," said the tall, stately Union officer as he walked through the door. Major Charles S. Jenkins, commanding officer of Ft. Rend, Tennessee, stood and saluted, then stuck out his to shake with his old West Point room mate.

"Good morning to you too, Colonel. Good to see you Frank. Been a while, but the years don't seem to have made much of a change on you," replied the Major.

"A few extra pounds, here and there, a little less hair, and I have to wear these damn reading glasses if the print isn't large. How about yourself, Charlie?" asked the Colonel.

The Major laughed and said, "More than a few pounds, I'm afraid, and the damn hair is just about gone. But the eyes are still holding up. After our duties out west, this desk job has been quite boring. But, if the rumors I'm hearing are true, that may all be about to change soon. And I take it your visit to my little fort has more to do with secessionists than socializing with old roommates. After receiving your telegram, I gave considerable thought to your request and think I have found just the man you will need. He was raised just south of here and has a good relationship with all of the local tribes, especially the Cherokee. He has worked as a liaison on numerous occasions, and speaks their language fluently. He is also anti-slavery and does not believe in the right of a state to secede from its' sovereign nation. I have not spoken to him much on the matter, as I understand the need for secrecy here. I will let you be the judge and decide if he is your man. Then you can fill him in on the rest."

The Major walked to the door and hollered for his aide. "Lt. Reed! Go and fetch Lt. O'Shea for me. He is over at the mess hall!"

"Frank, do you honestly think we can pull this off right here in the south and keep it quiet?" the Major asked, as he poured 2 shots of scotch, handing 1 to the Colonel.

"Well, Charlie, if we get to it as soon as the snow starts melting, hopefully we can have it all finished before any action takes place. I don't know all of the details as of yet, but the South Carolina congress has made it known that they will not brook any interference in their right to own slaves. And they have amassed quite a large militia. The secessionist movement is picking up steam, and there are rumors of several other states whose opinions are the same. The intelligence we have gathered indicate that Mississippi, Florida, Alabama, Georgia, and even North Carolina and Tennessee, may well side with South Carolina. But so far, none of them have done anything except voice their opinions in Congress. But our President has made it clear that he will not let the nation divide itself. Also, Tennessee seems to be evenly divided on the issue, with the western half of the state being pro-slavery due to all of the big farms and slave owners, while the eastern half is mostly small family farms. If we have to move spies and equipment clandestinely through these mountains at some point, we will need all of the intelligence we can get on the passes and trails through the upper elevations, and who better to guide us than the Indians? They ran us ragged for years disappearing into these mountains!" As he finished his explanation, Lt. O'Shea walked through the door.

"Lt. O'Shea reporting, sir." said the tall red-headed Irishman, as he snapped off a crisp salute.

"At ease, lieutenant. I would like you to meet an old friend of mine. We were roommates at West Point and served together in the skirmish with Mexico. Colonel Frank Piermont, of the Ohio 22nd, Army Intelligence," introduced the Major.

Lieutenant O'Shea saluted again, then stuck out his hand. "Good to meet you sir." he said.

The Colonel shook his hand and immediately liked what he saw. The lieutenant was a big man and had a hard, lean look about him, with piercing blue eyes that looked at the world from a face that carried crow's feet and the tan of a man use to living outdoors. He was probably younger than he looked, but he had an air about him that exuded confidence. As well as a combination of danger and humor, making the blue eyes dance when he became excited. All in all, the Colonel knew that before him stood a natural born leader, and the Major had made an excellent choice.

"My pleasure, Lieutenant. The Major has told me quite a bit about you, and seems to think you are the man I am looking for to carry out a very important mission, one that requires secrecy and the ability to communicate with the Cherokee. I understand that you speak several different dialects, and known to many of the tribes located in the mountain areas of North Carolina, Tennessee, and Alabama? And are on good terms with these tribes?"

"Yes sir," replied the Lieutenant, "Hope I can live up to the Major's praise, sir." "Well, you have no doubt heard of the secessionists movement being discussed in congress by several southern states. What I am needing from you, is to recruit as many Cherokee as you can to provide us with guides for our survey parties as they map routes through these mountain areas, and show us ways to move small units of men and supplies through them without being detected. I do believe there will come a time when this information will be quite important."

The Colonel walked over to a large table and cleared everything off of it, then began spreading out a number of maps.

"As you can see," he said, pointing to several areas circled in red, "we know very little about these mountains, except the major passes and trade routes. It could prove very beneficial for us to know how to get through these upper elevations undetected, as well as being able to stop anyone else from using them."

The Lt. examined the maps and started shaking his head. "Sir, are these the best you have? I myself can show you several ways through the Great Smokies at higher elevations that are not on these maps. And I'm sure the Cherokee know many more as far west as Chatanooga, and as far east as Asheville. But how long do we have? This is a huge area of very rugged country. Hell, Colonel, it would take 50 surveyors a year to cover this much ground!"

The Colonel scratched his head, looked at the maps again. "Lieutenant, I have 16 surveyors and at a guess, 12-16 months at the most, possibly less than that, and that's if we get started as soon as the snow starts to melt! And it must be kept quiet. The success of this mission will depend on its' secrecy. If word gets out, you and my surveyors will become the target of every secessionist and militia in 3 states! It will be quite an undertaking, Lieutenant, and depends entirely on your ability to recruit the right guides."

"I understand, sir. But it might not be as easy as you would like. The Cherokee have long memories, Colonel, and the forced march of 1838 to Oklahoma and subsequent treatment since have not left us in very good standing with them. I guess my next question is, what do we have to offer them for their services? What is it I can entice them with for their cooperation?" asked the Lieutenant.

The Colonel pulled a document from a waterproof case and spread it out on the table. "This hereby authorizes me to pay up to 100 dollars in 20 dollar gold pieces to each guide that successfully completes his mission, and, to offer them the return of some of their lands in Tennessee and North Carolina. It could turn out to be thousands of acres," he said.

"What do you think? Will that be enough to convince them to help us?"

"Yes sir, I think they may go for that, especially the land. The elders will go for that, and the gold will work for the younger braves who grasp the importance of gold in today's society. But I will need everything in writing, sir, and besides your surveyors, how many men may I take with me?"

"Choose your Indians well, Lt., for other than the surveyors they will be your only company. Officially, you are being re-assigned to me as an intelligence officer at Ft. McKinley, Ohio, with the 22nd Ohio, understand? After you have recruited your Indians, you will await the arrival of the surveyors here. Where you go from here, I will leave strictly up to you, as well as the pairing of the guides with the surveyors. All I require are updates every 30 days, and those are to be sent to the Major here. At the completion of your mission, I will make arrangements for the gold and deeds to be brought up from Atlanta. You can then deliver them to the

Cherokee. Any other questions for today, Lt.?" the colonel asked as he poured them all a drink.

O'Shea accepted his drink from the Colonel. "No sir. I think I understand what is required of me."

"Good, good. Meet me here at 0800 hours tomorrow, and we will discuss the money you will need to get this ball rolling. Dismissed, Lt."

The Lt. tossed back his drink, thinking 'this is my chance for a Captains commission, at least'. He snapped off a crisp salute, set his glass down and exited the Major's office.

"Well, Frank, what do you think? Was I right?" asked the Major.

"Yeah Charlie, I think he will do just fine!"

And with that, they raised their glasses and wished the Lt. the best of luck. Little did they know, he was going to damn well need it!

CHAPTER 5

THE SURVEYORS

L T. BRANDON O'SHEA had spit polished his boots, donned his dress uniform, trimmed his beard and cut his hair. He admired himself in the looking glass and imagined the Captains insignia upon his uniform. All he had to do was convince these 16 gentlemen to work with the Cherokee for one year. And likewise convince the Cherokee to do the same. 32 different personalities to pair up. How hard could it be?

The first to arrive had been John Charles Freemont. Even O'Shea had heard of him. Why, he had even run for president one time, been a state senator for California, and had surveyed half of the damn western states in his career! That he had been put in charge of this clandestine operation showed how important it was to the Colonel. He had long ago retired from the Army Corps of Engineers as a Colonel himself, and had now been re-instated as such again.

Officially, he was out west again on his 6th Western expedition, surveying for the railroad through the lower Rocky Mountains in Colorado and New Mexico. Surely, him being here would make his job easier, thought O'Shea, as Colonel Freemont was a proven leader of men and knew most of the surveyors. All the Lieutenant had to do was make sure he chose the right Indians to pair up with the Colonel's men.

The first of Colonel Freemont's surveyors to arrive was Claude Minot, a huge Frenchman that had been personally recruited by the Colonel, actually stolen away from George C. Swallow's private survey team out in

Arkansas. If he was any example of the surveyors Freemont was bringing in, O'Shea wasn't going to have to worry about their survival capabilities. He had worried that the surveyors would be a bunch of pencil pushing types from New York, and the Cherokee would be acting as baby sitters!

The young Lieutenant walked over to meet with both of the Colonels, as well as his commanding officer, Major Jenkins.

"Gentlemen," said the Major, "I would like to introduce you to Lt. Brandon O'Shea. He will be your liaison with the Cherokee. He speaks all the different tribal dialects, and knows the Indians well. He has arranged for 16 qualified guides who all speak enough English to get by. He will also be your go to guy for anything you need before leaving. And once the mission is finished, he will be the courier for the tribal payments."

O'Shea shook hands with all of the officers, then turned to Claude Minot and stuck out his hand. The big man looked O'Shea in the eye, then did his best to squeeze his hand in half. It didn't work. The Lieutenant matched the big mans squeeze pound for pound.

O'Shea even had a little left, but didn't want to make an enemy of the big guy.

"Damn, son, that's a hell of a grip ya got there!" exclaimed the Frenchman, and O'Shea knew he had just made a friend. But he wondered, who in the hell was he going to pair this guy with? Long Walker immediately came to mind. He was the biggest and oldest of the Cherokee, and also the smartest. Those 2 will make a hell of a team, he thought.

"And you sir, quite the grip yourself!"

"Ahh, hell, wished I was your age again," said Claude. "Gentlemen, please excuse us for a minute. The Lieutenant and I need to discuss some of the more necessary requirements I'll be needing before we start out. Lieutenant, after you," said the big man as he pointed toward the door.

As soon as they stepped outside, Claude asked him, "Mr. O'Shea, where might a thirsty fellow find a good red wine in these parts? I would be forever in your debt if you could find somewhere to procure a decent sweet red. I have with me 6 leather wine sacks I hope to fill before leaving on my journey, and as we may be gone for as long as 12 months, if you could find me a lass or 2 before then also?"

"Brandon, sir, or just Bran, if you wish. And we Irish have a knack for finding just such things. Once the parade of brass leaves, what say we take a stroll down to the far end of town?"

Over the next few days, the rest of the surveyors arrived, and the Lieutenant had to admit they were a tough and able looking crowd. No doubt that they should be able to handle their own with the Cherokee. No babysitting required. Bernard Fontaine, Chester Wright, and Caine Milsap had all been selected by the big Frenchman, while Rapheal Constantine, Joe Santavini, and Billy Blaine were from the Army Corps of Engineers. Nathan Carson, Hoyt Cordele, John Jackson, Clive Maxwell, and Bo Morgan had all worked with Colonel Freemont at one time or another and came well recommended. The remaining 3 had been recently working out west when summoned, and were the last to arrive. They were still dressed in western fashion when they arrived, buckskin jackets, leggings, wide brimmed hats and knee high boots. They were Teddy Simmons, Bob Calhoun, and Huston Fornetta.

After the arrival of the last 3, the following days were spent outfitting them all with everything they might possibly need, and selecting the areas for each individual to survey, and letting the Lieutenant get to know them a little. O'Shea already knew the different Cherokee guides that would be going. They were mostly a younger bunch of braves, except for Long Walker and 9 Toes. Brandon had known Long Walker longer than any of the rest, and knew that whoever he got paired with had better be a patient man! He was basically what a white man would refer to as a smart ass, while the Cherokee just thought him witty.

The Lieutenant's plan was simple by design. He would take the surveyors up to one of the deer camps and throw a big banquet, with venison, beef, turkey and hog. And of course, beer and wine. Hopefully, over the course of a couple of days of everyone getting to know each other, the pairing up would resolve itself naturally. The majority of the braves were between 25 to 35 years old. The plan was for the surveyors to explain which areas they had been assigned to, then find the guide who was most familiar with that area.

As for the surveyors, their ages ranged from 30 to 50, and there were 5 that concerned him. Claude Minot, the big Frenchman Brandon had gone drinking with, loved his wine, and the Lieutenant knew he had made arrangements to procure at least 4 gallons of the red. Brandon had also found out, that the more he drank, the louder he got, and the louder he got, the more vulgar he became, and would usually upset someone to the point of fighting. He was going to be difficult to pair with someone. Billy Baines was a very religious man and would preach and try to convert anyone who would stand still long enough. Whoever he paired with was going to have to listen to his sermons for 8 to 12 months. O'Shea knew that if it were he who was with him for that long, one of them wouldn't return!

Then there were the 3 who had arrived last, still dressed from working out west, where they had been under constant threat of Indian attacks from the Comanche, Apache and Kiowa. They just didn't like Indians, period, no matter what tribe or how civilized they were. It seems the Colonel had offered them extraordinary wages, but had failed to enlighten them to the fact they would be paired up with Indian guides! Upon finding out, they had threatened to leave, but somehow the Colonel had convinced them to stay. Brandon hoped that after a few days of associating with the Cherokee, that they would come to see what civilized people they were as compared to the savages out west.

The first day of the get together didn't go to badly, as the Lieutenant introduced the 2 parties and the 3 from out west were noticeably impressed by the Cherokee being so much different from the Indians they had been fighting. They made several comments to O'Shea that they wouldn't be a problem. The beer flowed, the wine flowed, everyone ate and a good time was had by all. The second day, however, wasn't quite as docile. It seems someone in the surveyors group had been talked into getting a few gallons of whiskey for the younger braves. So by the time the food was ready, everyone was to drunk to eat, and this resulted in wrestling matches, knife throwing contests and the big Frenchman chasing every female in the camp, regardless of ethnicity or marital status! And of course, Long Walker had to throw his 2 cents worth in, speaking only in Cherokee. That didn't work out to well, as Claude had worked in the Carolinas before and understood quite a bit of the language. So Claude decided to talk vulgar about Long Walker in French, as several of the surveyors spoke French. That didn't fare well either, for 9 Toes had worked with the French trappers up and down the Savannah River as a young brave and spoke fluent french, relaying everything the big guy said to Long Walker!

So during the knife throwing contest, Claude was to drunk to stand up, and threw from a sitting position and actually didn't do to bad. But when he tried to get up, he fell and landed in a prone position, which resulted in Long Walker making an amazing throw from 40 feet, landing only inches away from the crotch seam on the Frenchman's buckskin britches! Had Claude been able to get up, he would have tried to pound the Indian, but everyone was laughing so hard at his attempts to rise, that Long Walker escaped for the moment. Brandon just knew there was going to be a fight, if not a killing over the incident, but when Long Walker came back to retrieve his knife, he reached down and helped the Frenchman up! Claude actually handed him his knife and congratulated him on a very good throw!

On the 3rd day, O'Shea gathered the men up and read off the different areas to be surveyed. He was really surprised at the way the pairings had gone. Most of the Cherokee were familiar with all of the assigned areas, though some knew more about different parts of the mountains. One of the 1st surprises was Billy Baines, the preacher, and old 9 Toes. Neither of them drank and it seemed 9 Toes was interested in learning more about the Christian God he had heard about at the mission. After a few hours of comparing notes, just about everyone was teamed up with their counterpart. The only 2 left were Long Walker and the Frenchman. They stood there eyeing each other for several minutes, then Claude finally spoke in Cherokee.

"I guess I could partner up with someone who throws a knife so well. It took real skill not to hit the large package of manhood I carry!"

Everyone got a good laugh out of that, but O'Shea knew Long Walker well, and was not surprised at his answer.

"Being the excellent knife thrower I am, I took into consideration the little bump in the buckskins before I threw my knife. Wasn't much chance of hitting it"

And of course this also got a big laugh from those who understood Cherokee, but was even funnier when it had to be explained to those who didn't! Brandon figured that this would cause the fight avoided earlier, but was even more surprised when the 2 took off to the Cherokee village, where LongWalker claimed to know just the right widow for the Frenchman!

So it was, on April 1st, 1859 that the clandestine operation was set in motion. The promise of 100 dollars in gold coin to each of the participating braves and thousands of acres of land to the tribe was written into agreement and signed by both parties. The estimated time was to be 10 to 12 months at the most, and they were to meet at a secret location to be determined later.

CHAPTER 6

THE RECRUITMENT OF SGT. BURTON L. COMBS

July 1860

SERGEANT BURTON L. Combs, U.S. Army (ret.) and his wife Lena, sat on the front porch drinking tea and coffee, as was their morning ritual, and were discussing the upcoming days events around their farm. The 1,600 acres was under cultivation for corn, wheat, peach trees, and of course, cotton. The retired sergeant employed 6 full time farm hands, and when necessary, rented a few slaves from a neighbor during harvest.

Though he didn't personally own any slaves, he didn't think it was his place to tell another farmer how to run his farm. As he reached for the coffeepot, he noticed a dust cloud moving towards the entrance to his farm.

"Now who do you think this could be so early of a morn?" he asked his wife. He remained standing and looked to the rifle and pistol that lie on the bench, their usual place when he was at breakfast. His military background and the unrest of late had prompted him to start carrying his firearms again. As the carriage approached, he noticed it was being escorted by 2 soldiers dressed in South Carolina Militia uniforms. As the carriage drew up in front of the porch, his astonished eyes recognized none other than his former commanding officer, Major Albert G. Blanchard!

He exited the porch and stood at the stairs as the Major, dressed in civilian attire, pulled to a stop in front of him.

"As I live and breathe, if it isn't Big Al himself!" exclaimed the sergeant to his wife. The Major swung down with an ease that belied his true age. He held out both arms to engulf the sergeant in a bear hug that would have crushed a smaller man.

"Dammit, Burt, you look great! And what a spread you have here!" He turned to the 2 riders, "You boys water and feed the horses, please, while the Sergeant and I have a little chat. Then come on back as you have never tasted biscuits and red eye gravy like Mrs. Lena can cook! What do you say, Burt? Can a couple of old Indian fighters join you and I for breakfast?"

"It would be an honor, sir. Lena dear, you remember the Major from our trips to Charleston? My old commanding officer during the Mexican war, and my time out west? Why, we marched all the way to Vera Cruz together!"

"A pleasure to see you again, sir." replied Lena. "I have listened to many stories about ya'll's exploits in Mexico. It would be an honor for you to grace our table with your presence!"

"The honor is all mine, my dear. I have but one favor to ask of you. That I may speak privately with your husband for awhile, and that you not hate me afterwords?" asked the Major.

"Why of course, major. I'll get started whipping up some more gravy. You and Burt can have the porch all to your selves," Lena answered in her best Southern Belle charm. But Burton knew his wife well, and he noticed the look of concern cross her face as she exited the porch. The slam of the kitchen pantry echoed back, making both men wince a little. The sargeant turned to the Major.

"Sir, it really is good to see you, but what is it you actually came for? I know you didn't come all this way for a free breakfast and social call."

"No, Burt, I didn't. I'm sure you are just as surprised to see me, as I was to see Colonel Holmes when he arrived at my doorstep 2 weeks ago. You probably noticed that my escorts wear the Militia uniforms of South Carolina. They have been escorting me on my recruitment trips. I have made dozens of previous stops prior to coming here, and have requested of them the same thing I will be asking of you. So far, I have recruited 20 volunteers for you to choose from, should you agree to my request."

"I see. Well, Major, you have never been one to mince words, and I imagine with all of the latest unrest and talk of secession, that you are recruiting from your old division for the Militia. But how in the hell did you wind up here? Last I heard, you were living the retired life in Louisiana!"

"Ah, well, Burt, it is not that simple. I am still living in New Orleans, but I have agreed to a Colonel's commission here in the South Carolina Militia, particularly to oversee a very important mission of the utmost urgency. We have a mutual friend who has discovered a clandestine operation by the Union army to map all of the old Indian trails and passes through the mountains north of here, providing them with the means to infiltrate several states unknowingly, and the ability to move spies and supplies unseen. The Union has recruited the Cherokee as guides for their army surveyors, and now, after almost a year, we have information that they are finishing up. The Cherokee have retained possession of the maps, and are waiting on payment of gold and land deeds from the Union before relinquishing said maps to the army."

"Hold on a minute, uh, Colonel. Under whose authority are you assembling this unit? And who would be in charge, and who would be responsible for payment to my wife, should I agree?"

"As it stands, Burton, your commission would be reinstated as Sgt.1st Class, and you would receive the standard pay of 35 dollars a month, officially. But before I go into any further details, all I can say is that there would be a sizable bonus for each man if the mission is successful. But, I need your word and agreement, and a signature of oath before I can say more!"

The Sergeant scratched his head as a hundred questions flew through his mind. Did he really want to leave this docile existence on his farm? Just to go traipsing off into who knew what kind of dangerous adventure? He knew trouble was brewing in the South Carolina senate and the talk of possible war if they decided to leave the Union. He also had heard that there were several other states that would respond to South Carolina's actions by following suit. But so far, it had been just talk. And if war did break out, someone would definitely be coming to see him due to his military background. So, should he join now, and risk being a traitor to the Union, or be a patriot to his home state? If he got involved now and was caught, he could lose his farm at the least; at worst, be shot for a traitor. But life had become somewhat mundane, even boring, and he was still in good shape and relatively young, at only 33.

"How long, Colonel, would my services be needed for? And to whom do I report?" asked the Sergeant.

"You would be reporting to me, and be officially enlisted in the South Carolina State Militia for one year. But the mission I am requiring of you would need to take place as soon as we can put your unit together. If you sign today, I will fill you in on the particulars posthaste!"

"Okay, Colonel, let me think on this through lunch, and discuss it with my wife. I could certainly use the money, but I can't just be running off, and do need her blessing. If she agrees, then I'll take the mission, but only if I determine it to be accomplishable!"

"I understand, Burt, but you can't give her any details after I divulge them to you. Just that I have a very well paying job for you training men for the Militia, then you can explain it to her on your return."

After breakfast, the Colonel and his escort left for Anderson, leaving Burton with the unenviable task of explaining his reasons for leaving to Lena. She could tell his mind was made up, and knew he had already signed the commission. Argument was fruitless. He called Billy Hargrove to the porch and explained to him, as best he could, that he was now in charge of the farm. He would also receive a bonus for each crop successfully harvested. Lena would still run things, but Billy had been with them from the start 4 years ago, and knew as much as Burton about the farm.

The Sergeant explained to Billy that he was going to help train new recruits for the South Carolina Militia. He should be back in about 12 weeks. His wife knew it was a lie, but went along with the charade, thinking the extra money would go a long way on the farm. She hadn't just been idly sitting in the kitchen as her husband and the Colonel walked around the house. She had moved from room to room, as outside her husband and the Colonel circled the house discussing the mission. She had heard enough to know it involved an ambush and Indians. Enough to know that she wished she hadn't heard anything!

September 1860

The five men dressed in buckskins were all of similar build, and one look would tell you that they were at home in the mountains and forests.

They all had years of experience in the Indian wars out west, and 3 of them had also fought in the skirmish with Mexico. They sat closely together discussing the latest briefing with Colonel Blanchard. The mission seemed easy enough on paper, as if killing other men was ever easy. All that was required was that everything goes perfect. It could all be over in 2 weeks. But any military man with any actual experience knows that no plan ever goes perfect. So, they were discussing different options in case things went awry. Number 1, no matter what happens, the maps and deeds must not fall into Union hands. Number 2, they must not be taken captive. Number 3, they all wanted to live, so the plan must go as close to perfect as possible!

It was simple, really. They were to ambush the Union couriers and their escort, take from them the promised gold and land deeds, dress as the Union soldiers and proceed to the rendezvous. There, they were to exchange the gold and deeds for the maps and return to Anderson, where they would turn the maps over to Colonel Blanchard. Simple, right?

Now, after weeks of planning, they were heading out at sundown to travel through the mountains at night and be in position for the ambush in 5 days. The latest information from their spy at Ft. Rend, had the meeting set with the Cherokee at a hunting camp maintained yearly by the Cherokee. The couriers and their escort were coming from Atlanta with the gold and deeds, and were to meet with their liaison, a Lt. O'Shea, who would then lead them to camp near the village of Wilmot, in the Plotts Balsam mountains. All they had to do was find a good ambush spot somewhere along the Franklin Road.

CHAPTER 7

SEPTEMBER, 2007.
GRANDFATHER'S LODGE

DEUCE WALKED UP to the delicious aroma of bacon, biscuits and coffee. Grandfather was sitting out on the veranda enjoying his breakfast, so he sat down and joined him, asking if he had heard if Red was back yet.

"He called this morning and asked if you had any luck hunting. I told him yes, that you had some beautiful pictures of a magnificent buck that you didn't shoot. I said we were having Polaroid steaks, along with some pictures of beautiful biscuits and gravy. You will probably have to explain it to him later. He was confused. I did tell him that you still had your tracking skills, for I am sure you used them to get close for the pictures."

"Well, thank you for that," I laughed.

"Oh, no, I wasn't bragging on you. I was bragging on myself for being such a good teacher. If I was able to teach you such stealth, then I can teach anyone," he said.

"Well, uh, I am honored to have been taught by someone so humble," I managed to say, without choking on my biscuit.

"Are you going out again?"

"Yes sir, but not to hunt. I think I'll try to round up a metal detector and go back to that cave. Camp out for a few days, see what I can find. I am very curious to see what I can find in that canyon. Would you happen to know someone who might have one?"

He scratched his head, then said, "At the Cherokee Museum, you will ask for Yellow Wing. She is an old friend of mine. She is a historian for our people. Her family has been responsible for keeping our history for many generations. Legend has it, her family even helped Sequoya to create our written language. She is also a very highly regarded archi..uh..archio... dirt digger, too."

"An archaeologist?" I asked.

"Yes, that's it," he said. "I think you might like her, being all educated and such. She has more degrees than you, and like you, she uses her education to help her people. Only she doesn't charge nearly as much as you!"

I didn't know how to counter that remark without sounding like a capitalist, so I just finished my breakfast. By the time I was through, Grandfather was already into his after breakfast nap. I eased away from the table and was heading down the steps, when he opened one eye and said, "Red won't be back for 2 more days. Have fun at the Museum."

I took Red's jeep to the museum. I couldn't recall the last time I had been there. They were always adding to it and I was surprised to see how big it had become. Managing to look rustic, yet modern at the same time. It was no longer just a tourist trap, but an actual museum full of Cherokee and Indian history and artifacts. I walked up to a young man who was arranging an assortment of weapons in a display, and asked if Ms. Yellow Wing was around. He stuck out his hand and introduced himself as Ronnie Cloud, her assisstant, and asked who I was, so I used my official title, Deuce Hawkes, of Bruce, Fenton, and Hawkes, Legal Counsel for the Reservation, and mentioned that my Grandfather had sent to speak with Ms. Yellow Wing. He seemed duly impressed and said that he would go find her and inform her that I was here.

After her assistant had left to go find her, I began strolling through the exhibits, amazed at the life like wax statues and their realistic depiction of early Cherokee life. I was staring at one display of an incredibly beautiful Cherokee squaw standing in a hunting lodge scene. She was dressed in ceremonial buckskins and adorned with colored beads made of antler and bone, her hair in long braids that reached to her waist with feathers hanging from the braids. As I stared, the statue came to life and started walking towards me! At first I thought I was hallucinating, until she stopped in front of me and said, "Mr Hawkes? Hi, I'm Yellow Wing, the Museum curator. My assistant said you were here on some legal matter? How may I help you?" she asked, extending her hand.

Like an idiot, I just stood there for a second or two, then stuck my hand out also. It is hard to speak, even for a lawyer, with something as big as your heart stuck in the middle of your throat! I made some pitiful noise that sounded like a hurt puppy, took a deep breath and tried to regain my composure. Still in shock from seeing a statue come to life, I managed to shake her hand and mumble something that caused her to look at me and smile. I had a feeling that she was used to the effect that she had on the male population. She was most definitely not what came to mind when I thought of museum curators, or "old" friends of Grandfather's. I also had a feeling that I now knew why Grandfather has that sly look on his face when I had left!

"I'm sorry, I didn't mean to stare. But I thought you were part of the exhibit, so imagine my surprise when you started moving!" I stammered.

"Well, that means that either the statues are so life like that you could mistake them for real people, or I'm so waxy looking that you could mistake me for a statue," she said with a smile.

"No, no, I meant you were so beautiful standing there, I didn't think you could be real!" turning red as I said it, and causing her to blush slightly also.

"Why thank you, Mr. Hawkes. That is one of the more original lines I have heard in awhile. And believe me, I have heard a few. Now what can I do for you?" she asked.

Trying to regain my composure, I handed her a picture of the deer.

"I need a metal detector and my grandfather said I should ask you for one. I was hunting down south on the reservation when I spotted that magnificent creature, and began to track him and take pictures. While I was tracking him, he disappeared into a hidden cave that opened up into a box canyon. I followed him into the canyon, and while searching for him and exploring the canyon, I discovered 2 Civil War era bayonets making a cross high up in a tree! It seems apparent that they were placed there when the tree was quite small in order to mark a grave! Now, they are ten feet in the air, and only the tips and ends are sticking out. But under them, at the bottom of the tree, I found these!"

I pulled out the bandanna with the buckle and buttons wrapped in it. I laid them in her hand, and she began to study them closely.

"Come with me," she said, and I followed her through a sliding door, then down a long hallway to a set of double oak doors with large locks. She pulled out a set of keys and unlocked the door. As we entered, she began flipping light switches and lit up a cavernous room filled with artifacts, stuffed animals, and a weapons collection that lined the walls in every direction! There was one whole section of Civil War paraphernalia from both sides of the conflict, and even a couple of small cannons!

"Wow, this is some collection! I had no idea there was such an extensive collection here!" I said in awe. "As your legal rep, I suggest you get this inventoried and insured as soon as possible."

"Your grandfather called me right before you came and told me you were on the way. He and I are old friends. He wasn't too sure what you wanted the detector for. I guess you haven't shown these to him?"

"Not yet. There is some more stuff, too, but I took them to a professor friend of my Dad's at the University. Seems it was an old map case full of documents and had to be opened in their special climate controlled room."

"Well, the Cherokee people have been bringing in the items they find for over a hundred years. Most of it was just crammed into an old longhouse until we built this new addition. Quite a bit of it is still in fair to bad shape, but profits from the casino have allowed me to hire extra help to start cleaning and documenting it all. We will be displaying some of it in the future, but we still have a long way to go. There may even be some legal issues on a few things, rights of ownership, which is why I agreed to show it to you. But for now, lets go look at our buckle, button, and medals collection."

We turned down another aisle and I spotted a small glass room with all types of hoses and wires running to it. It was a smaller version of the dry vault at the University.

"I notice you have a dry vault also. Why do you need one here?" I asked.

"Some of the tribal records are written on animal hides and would deteriorate if not stored and handled properly. And we have many old diaries and journals. You'd be surprised at how many people chronicled their participation in the war. I guess everyone understood how historic the events of the time would be and wanted to document their efforts, regardless how trivial it seemed at the time. We have hundreds of letters, copies of orders issued by one command or the other, as well as tribal records of our people's involvement. Some for the South, some for the North. The Cherokee tried to remain neutral as a tribe, but the war went on for so long and there were many individuals who assisted one side or the other for their own reasons. Here we are," she said, and pointed to a glass case full of buckles and buttons.

She laid the buttons on a blue cloth under a large magnifying glass that was mounted on a stand with a strong light.

"The design stayed pretty much the same for the Union buttons through out the war, but in the south, as the war went on, they stopped using brass and went to tin. They needed the brass for munitions casings. So, by comparison of weight alone, I should be able to approximate their age," she said, as she began to examine them.

"These are pretty early in the war. Look closely and you can tell the craftsmanship was first rate, with tiny little ornamental feathers, barely visible now. And they are bigger and heavier than later years. The buckle, too."

She slipped on a pair of white cotton gloves, and handed me a pair. She opened one of the cases and pulled out a tray lined with buttons.

"See these? Feel how much lighter and smaller they are?"

"So these came from when, 1861 or so?" I asked.

"What makes you think these are Confederate?" she asked.

She examined them again, then pulled out a tray of buttons from Union coats. There were some with identical markings, some with just US on them, and some with initials representing divisions from different states. I looked at the buttons closely and said "Well, the buckle has CSA on it, so I just assumed the buttons were Confederate also."

She took the buckle and laid it on a blue felt pad and switched on a light powerful enough to start a fire with. She opened a small vial and began to swab some type of cleaning solution on the front of the buckle, where I was sure the CSA initials would show up. We were both taken by surprise when the initials turned out to be SCSM.

Puzzled, she said, "I'm not sure what these letters stand for. Lets look at the back now. Sometimes they would engrave their name and rank on the back so as not to get them mixed up in the camps or barracks. Or, for ID purposes in case they were killed."

She began rubbing the solution on the back of the buckle. Standing there next to her, I could smell the flowers in her hair and the aroma of tanned leather. What a combination!

"When my grandfather said you were an old friend, I had thought the key word was 'old'," I said.

She laughed and said, "Well, he was there when I was born, so how many years do you have to know someone before you can call them an old friend? My father and he were also good friends, and they were 30 years apart."

"But if you were around all of this time, I would have remembered you. I would have seen you at sometime or another. And I wouldn't forget someone as, uh, well I mean, we would had to have met," I stammered.

"Oh, but Mr Hawkes, we did! In fact, you and that ornery cousin of yours took my horse one time while I was digging for old beads, and I had to walk 5 miles home crying all the way! And then there was the time when one of you cut the rope swing nearly in 2, and it was Doe Eyes and I that swung next and it broke, dumping us into the creek! And it was so cold!"

She turned and looked me in the eyes, and I remembered it all as if it were yesterday! Sparrow? No! This can't be her! With the buckteeth and the skinny legs and always had dirt on her from climbing trees or digging in the dirt! But she was so much younger than us, or so it seemed back then!

"Well, well, I do remember now! Little Sparrow! And you were always digging up little trinkets and artifacts you just had to show us. No wonder you became an archaeologist! So, you took Yellow Wing as your woman's name?"

She smiled at me over her shoulder and said, "Look here, there is your answer."

The buckle was inscribed with Sgt. Burt Combs 1860. I didn't want to spoil the moment by telling her that I already knew who he was. She walked over to the computer and typed in the SCSM inscription. Up came an emblem and the words, South Carolina State Militia.

"Now what in the world was he doing in that canyon that got him killed?" she asked. "I don't know yet, but if you'll loan me a metal detector I'm going to go back and see what I can find. I also need to go back by UT and see what they have come up with from the map case and documents they found in it."

"Sure. Right over here." She walked over to a cabinet and unlocked it, pulling out an expensive looking piece of equipment. "Just be careful with it. It's a top of the line unit, costing about 5000 dollars. Here, take the instruction booklet, too."

"Uh, Yellow Wing, how would you like to come with me and run this thing? You know more about this kind of thing than I do, and its' a beautiful ride down there to the canyon?"

"Why, Deuce Hawkes, is that your way of asking me out on a date? You sure know how to excite a girl! Asking her to go digging up old bones and playing in the dirt! And while that is one of my favorite hobbies, I'm afraid I'll have to pass. I'm leaving for Oklahoma shortly for a gathering of historians from the 5 civilized tribes of the east. I was going to leave earlier, but after Grandfather called, I couldn't miss the chance to see the look on your face when you found out who I was!"

"Okay, you got me there. And I'm sure this is all going to be real funny to Grandfather. But how about when you get back?" I asked, trying to sound sincere.

"We'll see, Mr. Hawkes, we'll see. But for now, I must get going if I am going to catch my flight."

The fog lay heavy on the ground as I pulled away from the stables. I had loaded up the piebald mare again, plus an older mare for a pack horse. I had enough supplies to last for quite awhile, planning to stay at the cave for 3 or 4 days at least. I stopped at the cabin and unloaded the horses from the trailer. I saddled the paint and loaded provisions and 5 gallons of water on the old mare. The rest of the food and gear I left in the cabin, along with a note and map showing Red where I had gone.

The ride through the mountains was even more scenic now. I rode slowly, examining the shadowy areas even more closely. The knowledge, or lack of, about what might lie hidden in these canyons now haunted me. Any dark space along the face of one of the granite monoliths drew my attention. What might lie hidden in some cave or canyon in this desolate area was feeding my curiosity and imagination. And even knowing where the valley and canyon were at, it still took 2 tries to find it again. I dismounted and led the horses through the brush. Nearly to the entrance, both horses began to act up, pulling me backwards as they decided to exit the brush in reverse. I led them back out of the brush and tied them tightly to a tree. I grabbed my shotgun, checked my .357 mag pistol and eased into the bushes a little more cautious this time. It took only a few steps towards the entrance to the cave to discover the reason for the horse's actions. It seems I hadn't been the only visitor recently. Several large tracks led into and then back out of the cave. I squatted down for a closer look and determined it was a large bear. 1 large enough so that my hand fit right inside of the bear's track.

I eased on into the cave and followed the tracks out into the canyon. After about 75 feet in, the tracks stopped, turned about face and went right back out through the cave. For whatever reason, the bear had decided that this canyon wasn't the place for him! I went and got the hoses and led them more slowly this time, keeping up a soft, constant, conversation with them, but they were still a little skittish. The good thing was that the bear was not in the area, or they would never have let me lead them in. I got the horses unloaded and went about setting up my camp and gathering firewood. While doing so, I remembered a little trick Grandfather had taught me about setting animal alarms around your camping area. I emptied the contents of several cans of soup into the cook pan, then took some rope and tied the cans on close enough to each other so that any disturbance of the rope would cause the cans to hit each other. I then drug a bunch of large limbs up to the front entrance and piled them there with the rope running through them. I shook the branches and the cans rattled just loud enough to get my attention should anything try and enter. I then cooked up the soup, ate, and began to unwrap the metal detector and tools I brought. I had spent the previous evening reading all about the functions of the detector.

All of the different beeps it makes to indicate different metals, depths, etc. I walked to the back of the cave and started against the far wall, working my way to the front. After about 5 minutes, the detector let out a screeching beep that literally caused me to jump sideways. I turned the volume down immediately.

Now, with my heart still racing, I dropped to my knees and began digging with the small garden spade, and using the hand held probe to search each clump of dirt. The cave floor was packed pretty solid and it took a few minutes to get deep enough to find the objects. At first, I had no idea what I had unearthed. It was just a large glob of metal about the size of a golf ball. I looked at the detector to see what metal it had responded to. Lead, and the clump of metal looked more like a melted cluster of grapes. Lead shot! Cap and ball type ammo! I sat them aside and probed the hole again and it kept beeping, so I dug the hole wider and deeper. A long cylindrical item was the next thing I found. It was obviously a gun barrel, but so rusted it was coming apart as I tried to dig it out. I finally managed to get it out in four different pieces.

The next discovery didn't respond to the metal detector, and my attempt to dig them up was causing them to fall apart. They were definitely bones! But were they human? I began to wonder if the pistol might have had a hand around it as it sank into the ground? And was the rest of the body beneath me also? I piled the little bones up on a piece of plastic and probed the hole some more, this time getting a different sounding beep. One that indicated gold! I dug and probed and dug some more until I found a small circular gold ring. Wiping it clean, it was clear that it was a simple gold wedding ring! I sat the ring on the plastic sheet with the bones and rested against the wall.

I took a drink of water and thought to myself, Deuce, you are way out of your league here, man. I was probably doing more harm than good to the site. I knew that the more I dug, the more bones I would find, and I had no idea how to do it properly. Then I remembered that finding human remains had to be reported to the authorities. I turned the detector off, got up and brushed off my jeans. I walked out of the cave and checked on the horses, trying to decide what to do. The smart thing would be to load up in the morning and head back to the reservation. Then contact the professor and ask him how to proceed. But I just couldn't resist taking the detector over to the 'bayonet tree' and see what I could find there!

At about 10 feet from the tree, I took a stick and marked off an area roughly 20 feet by 20 feet. I turned the detector on and began sweeping the area as I walked towards the tree. At about 5 feet, it began making a high pitched squeal that I now recognized as either lead or steel. I stopped where it indicated and began digging again. This time, at around 18 inches deep, I recognized the metal tube as another gun barrel. I just left it there, and dug some more, a little closer to the tree. The hand unit beeped again, showing lead or brass, and I dug until I hit something large and round. When I cleaned around it, I recognized a human skull. I managed to dig completely around it and lift it out in one piece. There was a hole in the left side of the temple, and a larger one in the rear of the skull! Okay, that's it! I decided right then that I had had enough grave robbing! I wrapped the skull in a towel and put it with the other things I had discovered. Returning to the cave, I began to pack up my gear and get ready to leave at first light. All I had to do now, was spend the night in a cave of dead men.

CHAPTER 8

SGT. COMBS JOURNAL

FTER A NIGHT of tossing and turning in the cave, my sleep haunted by my imagination, I was more than happy to see the sun come up. After loading the horses and leading them through the cave, I replaced the cut branches in front of the cave to help conceal the entrance. I had been riding for about an hour when I crested a large hill and began hearing a beeping noise coming from my saddlebags. At first, it was such a strange sound in all of this natural serenity. Then I remembered stuffing my cell phone in there. I had no idea it would work out here in the middle of nowhere, then I realized how high above the canyon and valley I had ridden.

"Hello?"

"Mr. Hawkes? Professor Hartshorne here young man! I hope I didn't disturb you calling so early, but I have some interesting news for you! We have completed the task of piecing together the rest of the papers and the Sergeant's journal that was in the map case, and my research team have made some very puzzling discoveries regarding him and his men. I could tell you all about it, but it would take too long. Better that you come to Knoxville and read them for yourself!"

"Yes sir, Professor. I was just leaving the cave site, and have found some more artifacts, as well as bones and a skull. At this stage, I decided it would be better to bring you or one of your assistants back with me, or maybe Ms. Yellow Wing from the reservation, who is also an archaeologist. I can be there tomorrow around noon, if that's a good time for you?"

"Yes, yes, noon will be just fine. So, you have met the beautiful Ms. Yellow wing? We have met on several occasions, a most delightful and intelligent young lady. Tell me, young man, is this site actually on reservation land?"

The question took me by surprise, as I wasn't sure that it was. But before I showed anyone exactly where it was, I needed to know for sure whose land it was on.

"Yes sir, I'm pretty sure it is. But for now, I still have an hour or so ride to the cabins, then a hard drive back to the reservation. I will see you tomorrow, sir."

I sat before my Grandfather at the table, where for the better part of an hour I had been explaining to him my adventure up to now. I read to him the few pages that I had obtained from the Professor on my first visit to the university, and told him what Yellow Wing and I had determined from the buckle and buttons. When I finished, I thought he might have dozed off, for he stayed quiet for so long.

"Grandfather? What do you think?" I asked. Still silence. "Grandfather?"

"You ask what I think? I think you sat up there in your fancy office for the last five years, then you come back into a world you had lost interest in. But it seems obvious that this world has not lost interest in you. It seems that it must be time for this story to be told, and the spirits have chosen you to tell it. Why now, and why you, are the questions you should be concerned with!"

"There may be some record of this legend in the old tribal documents. It would not surprise me to find out that the Elders had made some kind of deal with the Yankees back then, especially if there was land involved. They actually didn't care who won the war, and for awhile we thought that they might kill each other off. But as more died, more just kept coming.

Yellow Wing is back, and should be here any time now. You go with her and she will show you things in the archives not meant for display. There are many things in there that are not meant for white men's eyes, so you must read them with your Cherokee eyes only. Or have her read them to you. Good luck with that," he said, as he went out on the porch. He walked back in escorted by Yellow Wing. This time, instead of the ceremonial style buckskins, she was dressed as a businesswoman, in a dark blue, knee length skirt, and matching vest over a light blue shirt. Her hair was still adorned with beads, down to her waist, and if anything, was even more beautiful than the first time I met her!

"Quit staring and say something educated," said Grandfather. "I like to hear what comes out when young men try to speak to her. Pitiful little noises. Sounds like frogs choking. Try saying your own name first, then graduate to 'Good Morning, Miss Wing," Grandfather advised, laughing as he headed for his room.

I laughed along with him, remembering my first meeting with her. Much more confident now, I said "Good morning Ms. Yellow Wing. I feel I have regained my composure enough not to stutter at meeting you."

She laughed and smiled at me, and I knew that if I said anything right then, it would be worse than the first time, as her laughing smile had left me mute!

"Good morning to you too, Deuce. Grandfather says you have some documents for me to read and some interest in reading some old tribal records? Lets drink some of his delicious coffee while I read what you brought, then we'll head over to the archive vault and see what we can find."

I handed her the papers and went to pour some coffee. As I passed by Grandfather's room, I noticed his eyes were closed, but I knew his ears weren't! When I returned with our coffee, she was staring at the box on the floor. I had forgotten about it!

"And what did you discover with the metal detector? More good stuff?" she asked as she reached for the box.

"Wait, not here. Let's take it to the museum and examine the contents there!" I said. "Well, alright" she replied, giving me a puzzled look. I didn't want Grandfather knowing I had brought a dead man's bones into his lodge, especially a white man's bones! I'm sure there was some evil spirit or another that would cause him to perform some type of cleansing ritual over it, and I was running out of time. It was already after 8:00 am and I still had a two hour drive to Knoxville before noon.

When we stepped outside, I explained to her why, and she gave me a stern look.

"You know that when you find human remains, you aren't supposed to move them until they have been examined by the authorities! What if it turns out that they aren't 159 years old, but only 5 years old?" she asked.

"Yeah, I thought about that ten minutes after I had already dug them up. But with the rest of the stuff, it is pretty obvious that the graves are not recent, "I explained.

"Graves? As in more than one?" she asked.

"Uh-huh. As in more than one. But one seemed to have only an arm and hand and gun in it. I'm thinking that maybe an animal drug the arm off and years of sediment had covered it up."

At the museum, she spread out a towel and we both donned the white gloves and removed everything from the box. At first she was ecstatic about the pistol, until she seen what I mess I had made of it digging it out. She then identified the lead mass to be the pistol ammo I thought it was. The gold ring nearly brought tears to her eyes. She placed it to the side and looked at the small bones, identifying them as finger bones, and the large bone as the ulna or arm bone. She carefully unwrapped the skull, holding it in such a way that the jawbone didn't move or try to come off. She began to take pictures of it, and measure the size of the entrance wound and exit wound.

"This was done from awfully close. Maybe even pressed against the temple, possibly self inflicted," she explained.

"Okay. That would make sense, what with the cross of bayonets and all. If you would carefully wrap the skull back up, I'll take it with me when I go see Professor Hartshorne. In fact, I'm supposed to be there at noon. Would you like to come with me? He has finished piecing together the rest of the journal and has apparently found some interesting details."

"I know the professor well. A very talented and respected archaeologist, and so is his assistant, Carrie. But one thing you haven't told me. Are you sure this canyon and cave are on reservation land?"

"Uh, well, I think so. I know the cabins are, and they're about 2 hours by horseback from the canyon, roughly 6-7 miles. Why does everybody keep asking me this?"

She shook her head and laughed. "You're supposed to be a lawyer and you don't realize the implications of where the site is located? If it is not on the reservation, then it is on federal or private land. Either one and you were trespassing when you discovered it and we have no claim to it what so ever! So let's hope that you were still on the reservation! If it is on federal land, then your friend at the university will file an archaeological claim and take all of this away from us!"

God, I felt like such an idiot! That should have been the first thing I checked before talking to Professor Hartshorne. I had gotten so caught up in the adventure that I hadn't even thought about the ramifications of it not being on the reservation! If anyone would know, It'd be Red Legs, and he was due back today.

"Red will know. He is the one who told me where to hunt. And I haven't told anyone where it's at, though the professor did ask. I was going to GPS it, but my phone only works until about 3 miles from the cave."

She started her head shaking and laughter again. "Red? That crazy fool has hunted deer all over Tennessee and North Carolina, never caring if he was on the reservation or not. He'd kill one 20 miles away and drag it back, then tag it! And those cabins? You boys weren't the only ones who would sneak down there to party! They are as far south as the reservation goes. If you turned back due east, you were not on the reservation, but directly northeast and you would have been. Don't tell anyone until we can get a GPS fix for real and see. Especially not the professor's assistant Carrie!"

Wow, I really made a good impression on her! What a dumbass! Hopefully I could fix it when we found out it is on the reservation!

"So, do you want to come with me?"

"Sorry, Deuce. I can't. I have a hundred things to do today. Well, a hundred and one, if you want me to find time to look in the archives. So many of the old records have not been entered into the computer yet and will have to be researched and read physically from the notes. It will take both of us days to go through the ones for 1859-1860."

"Mr. Hawkes! How very good to see you again," said the professor as he shook my hand. "We have so very much to show you, that I really don't know where to start! We have researched the backgrounds of all of the names we discovered, and a very puzzling story has unfolded! Something of a mystery, I assure you!"

He led me into a classroom where there were piles of papers stacked on large tables. "Let's start with the Major Blanchard mentioned in the first legible entry of the journal. He shows up in the Mexican-American war, then retires to and doesn't show up again until the Civil War as a commissioned officer, a Brigadier General in the Confederate army. He was commanding the 1st Louisiana Infantry regiment, deployed to Virginia where his brigade is posted at Portsmouth, Virginia. His brigade was at the Battle of Seven Pines, but held in reserve. After that, he was replaced by General Ambrose R.Wright because of his advancing age. It seems that General Lee desired a younger officer to lead in the field. He goes on to serve in the Louisiana Senate after the war. But there is no mention of him ever being involved with the Sgt. Nor any mention of the mission he sent the Sgt. and his men on," explained the professor.

"What about Sgt. Combs? Are there any records of him being in the South Carolina Militia? I asked.

"Ah, well, unfortunately, the only records we have for him are his years in the U.S. Army prior to, and during the Mexican-American war. There was a land grant and purchase title that shows his wife passing away and the farm being bought by William Hargrove, then later confiscated by the Union for his participation in the war. There are no records, military or otherwise, of the Sgt.'s mission or his return. But once you read the rest of the journal, you'll understand why."

As they entered the room adjoining the documents vault, Deuces heart began to race as he spotted the transcripts magnified on the whiteboards that covered the walls. He handed the box with his latest finds to the professor's assistant, and explained what was in it and his thoughts on the bullet hole in the skull. The young man left quickly, eager to examine the latest finds. The professor then led him to the far corner of the room and pointed his laser at the earlier documents, rehashing the story from the start, and leading up to the latest renderings. How they had managed to decipher the blood smeared handwriting of the last few pages was something of a miracle in itself.

"Let's begin with what we already have determined, just for presentations sake," said the professor. "The first document is a list of the men assigned to Sgt. Combs. As you know, we first thought they were Confederate soldiers, but couldn't find any records for them. After we discovered they were U.S.Army personnel and coming from the Indian wars out west, and also the date being 1859-1860, we have found some info on them as to their military service, but once again, only up to 1860. After that, nothing! But the Sgt.'s journal does explain what happened to them. But I'm not going to spoil it for you. I'll let you read what we have compiled for yourself. At the end, you'll most likely agree that there must be many more map cases buried somewhere, and they'll need to be discovered if we are ever going to know the full story!"

The first page I read was the letter from the spy who was keeping tabs on the surveyors and Lt. O'Shea. Seems that he was Cherokee. He had listed in detail that there were over 60 maps to be delivered and even where and when the rendezvous was to take place. He even knew where the couriers with the gold were to meet the Lieutenant. This explained where the Sgt.'s information had come from, but of course didn't mention the Cherokee's name. Would love to know that, I thought. The second page was a set of deployment orders and mission criteria explaining the basics of the mission and giving command of said mission to Sgt. Combs. All of the remaining pages were from Sgt. Combs journal. I had already perused the first few entries earlier, as they were the most easily legible. But I wanted to keep the whole story in perspective, so I began at the beginning.

April 2nd, 1860

I am Sgt.1st Class Burton L. Combs, brought out of retirement by my old friend for a clandestine mission, involving myself and 4 other men. I am writing in this journal in the hope that someone will discover it if I am captured or killed, and my wife will know what happened to me if I don't return. We were sworn to secrecy and couldn't tell anyone where we were going or why. The 4 men with me were handpicked by my old commanding officer for their expertise at moving undetected through most any terrain. They are all veterans of the Indian wars out west, and are accomplished woodmen, as am I. Their names are listed here, but I was never told what ranks they held. Only their ages and years of service. I am assuming they must all have achieved the rank of sergeant due to their years of service. Damien Carter, 32, whom I have assigned as my second in command, Clancy Moore, 31, Gerwin Upshaw, 33, and Daniel Desmond, 29. All have at least 7 years of service or more, and are secessionist sympathizers from southern states. We have been brought together under unusual circumstances, and now, after a month together, have formed a bond of trust in each other. Such a bond is necessary for a mission like this to be successful.

His next entry was April 3rd, and was just a few personal notes on each man. He had taken a liking to the youngest, Desmond, and spoke highly of him. The 2 older men, Upshaw and Moore, had been serving together for several years and came as a set, keeping mostly to themselves, while Carter seemed to be the loner of the group.

The 3ʳᵈ entry was on April 6ᵗʰ, and described the preparations for the upcoming ambush.

I sent Upshaw and Moore ahead to scout out a likely ambush area. We knew from which way the couriers would be coming, led by their escort, a Lt. Brandon O'Shea. Our intelligence report said that there would be 2 couriers, and a 4 man security team, making a total of 6 armed men. Moore reported back that he had found the perfect location, and Upshaw had remained to watch the area. We followed Moore back to the ambush location, and I had to admit, it was the perfect kill zone. The trail narrowed as it approached a small creek crossing, leaving us the high ground above the trail. We would be able to catch them in a crossfire from the elevated vantage point, shooting down into the low water crossing. We then moved the horses to a safe distance, about ¼ of a mile away. I sent Upshaw back down the trail to watch for the approaching soldiers. His ability to move soundlessly at night further enforced my opinion that the Major had chosen well. We now had less than 72 hours to accomplish step 1 of our mission, and prepare to meet the Cherokee.

April 7

I was standing watch when Upshaw returned, sometime around midnight. He informed me that the Union soldiers were camped approximately 3 miles down the trail and would most probably be moving out at sunrise. I then sent Carter back to watch the trail above us for any unwanted visitors, and sent Moore south to watch the Union men. Upshaw, Desmond, and I, tried to get what sleep we could, but I doubt anyone slept. As the first gray light of dawn appeared, Moore returned, saying the couriers and party were breaking camp, and should be here within the hour. Moments later, Carter arrived to assure me the horses were safe, and there was no one else around. In a matter of minutes, everyone was in position except me, as I had to brush the ground with branches and make the area look undisturbed. I brushed my own tracks to my tree, then climbed into position. We were now set.

One hour after sunrise, we could hear them talking and riding slowly, telling jokes and laughing. And why not, for they were totally unsuspecting of any danger this close to their destination. As they entered the kill zone they were being led by a big red headed man. I assumed he was the lieutenant I had heard about. He suddenly became wary of the water crossing, maybe even realizing what a perfect place for an ambush it was. Instead of leading everyone into the kill zone, he stopped and began to look around. When he scanned the trees above him, his eyes met mine as I fired! A thunderous volley rang out from the surrounding trees as the cries of pain and startled horses interrupted the peaceful morning! Within minutes, six men and one horse lay dead, their blood mingling with the water in the creek. We descended from the trees and began gathering up the horses. It was then, as the ringing in my ears subsided, that I heard Desmond calling my name. I turned to see him holding Carter's head in his lap, even though it was obvious he was dead. I couldn't believe my eyes! Everything had gone just as planned. I didn't think the Union boys had even gotten off a shot! But dead he was! Moore and Upshaw had by now gathered the horses, and also discovered one courier who was only wounded. Before I could determine what to do with him, Upshaw slid his knife from its sheath and cut his throat! Another reminder that these were seasoned Indian fighters and had no qualms about killing!

We began stripping the dead men from their uniforms. I had told them all to try for head shots as not to put any holes in the uniforms. In this we were pretty much successful and what blood there was, we washed out in the cold water of the creek. We then drug the bodies down a few hundred feet and placed them beneath an overhang of rock and dirt, allowing us to dig beneath it until it collapsed and covered them. We then buried Carter's body and said a few words over him. After that, we lead the captured horses over to where ours were hidden. We began swapping out our horses for theirs, due to the fact that all army horses have the US branded on both hips.

After patching a few bullet holes and letting them dry from the washing in the creek, the uniforms actually fit quite well. The only uniform that couldn't be used was the lieutenant's, for he had been much bigger than any of us. Unfortunately, we now didn't need but 4 anyway. The 1st step of our mission was complete.

Deuce sat back and tried to comprehend what it took for men to shoot someone, then strip the dead and wear the clothes of the men you just killed! He looked at the next entry of the Sergeant's journal, dated April 8th, the day of the rendezvous with the Cherokee, and knew that the next pages would only contain more death.

CHAPTER 9

SERGEANT COMB'S
JOURNAL, PART 2

*B*EFORE LEAVING OUT *this morning, I did a thorough inventory of all of the belongings of the Lieutenant and his entourage. I discovered a strongbox with a double sided padlock, thinking this was surely where the gold was kept. After finding a set of keys on one of the couriers, I opened the box while Upshaw and Moore reloaded the pack horse and US horses with our gear. We released our horses and let them run free.*

Inside the box was a matching pair of Colt Navy Dragoons, .38 caliber pistols, and I must say that I have never seen a finer set of handguns! Pearl inlaid handles with fine silver scrolls etched into the chambers and barrels! An inscription on the butt of the first pistol read, "To Lt. O'Shea, From a Grateful Nation". The second one read "To Longwalker, From a Grateful Nation". They lay wrapped in silk in a molded leather tray.

Also in the box, was an envelope containing the titles and property deeds to thousands of acres of land that had been signed over to the Cherokee, and a small pouch containing some silver coins and some paper cash, but no gold. Desmond was beside me rummaging through another pack, and discovered 10 bottles of good Tennessee whiskey. We had brought a few bottles ourselves, but this additional 10 assured us that we had enough to inebriate what I hoped were only a few Indians. I instructed Desmond to pour out half of the whiskey in our bottles, and fill them back with water, allowing us to drink with the

Indians. I began searching the other bags for the gold, and told Desmond to load the gun box back onto the pack horse. He asked me If I had noticed how heavy the box was, containing only 2 pistols and some coins? He sat it back down and I re-opened it and removed the pistols and envelopes. I used my knife to pry around the edges of the pistol tray, and sure enough, it lifted out revealing a false bottom. I pried the boards loose and discovered a hidden compartment. It contained 16 blue velvet pouches, each one containing 5 twentydollar gold pieces. Nearly 6 year wages to a common soldier! I quickly re-inserted the bottom board and gun tray, locked the strongbox back up, and loaded it on the pack horse! I looked at Desmond and told him that this would be our little secret as to how much was here. Just for the time being. I didn't want my men to kill the Cherokee just for the gold. The plan was still to buy the maps from them and avoid a skirmish.

After erasing all evidence of our presence, we traveled day and night to reach the rendezvous point, a small encampment by the river. I had explained several times to my men what our plan of action would be, depending on the number of Indians present at the encampment. I, and they, knew that nothing ever goes as planned and we must be ready to improvise.

It was nearly 2 o'clock when we were approached by 2 Cherokee braves, emerging from the trees to escort us. As we entered the encampment, I began counting the number of Indians, and was relieved to find only 6 there. The largest and eldest of the bunch was standing in front of a lodge pole and mud hut. As I rode up to him, the first thing he asked was, where is Lieutenant O'Shea? I explained to him that duty had called him to be elsewhere and that I, Sergeant Ames, which was on my uniform, was his replacement. I then asked, "Which of you is Longwalker?" The same tall Indian tapped his chest and said it was he. I have a gift for you from the lieutenant, I told him, then dismounted. I had taken the pistols out and hid the lieutenant's in the bottom of my saddlebag, while leaving Longwalker's wrapped in oilskin and riding on top in the bag. I pulled the pistol out and handed it to the big Cherokee. He accepted the weapon and began to admire its' craftsmanship, then read aloud the inscription. Thank you, he said, and motioned for us to follow him.

"You may camp there by the fire," he said. I ordered my men to unload the pack horse of food and whiskey, while Longwalker and I walked along the

river bank. "You have the gold?" he asked. "Yes, of course," I answered, "And you have the maps?"

"Yes", he replied, "And you also have the land deeds for us, too?"

"Yes, I do. Shall we eat and drink a bit, then make the exchange?" I asked.

"Bring the gold and deeds to the front of my lodge and we will exchange after we feast. There are 16 map cases the Lt. O'shea gave us. Each case contains 6 maps. You will give me the gold for all 16 braves who worked for your surveyors, even though 2 of them did not return. The gold will go to their families. This was reported to the Fort. The 2 surveyors with them did not return either." He then turned and walked away, admiring his new pistol.

I walked back to my men as they unloaded the gifts and whiskey for the Cherokee. They sat the whiskey beneath a small tree and invited the Indians to help themselves. We began to join them, drinking from our watered down supply. I had instructed the men to leave our horses saddled for the time being. They were to react to my actions, as I didn't really have a plan set in stone, and was just going to wait until I deemed an appropriate time to engage the Indians. We sat among them in front of Longwalker's lodge and feasted on venison and turkey, as well as much whiskey. All except Longwalker. When I offered him a drink, he politely refused and said that he had learned a long time ago what kind of fool he became when drinking whiskey. He did like beer, and wine also, but not whiskey. A few minutes later he and a young brave exited his lodge carrying the 16 map cases. They laid them on a blanket between us. I sat the strongbox between us and opened it up, removing the gun tray and prying out the false bottom. Longwalker noticed the tray was made for 2 guns and asked, "Who has the other gun?" I explained that it had been given to Lieutenant O'Shea and was inscribed similarly to his. As I began to remove the pouches of gold, I noticed Moore and Upshaw staring at it intently, this being the first time they had seen how much gold was actually there. I opened each pouch and showed him the coins, and he sat them next to the maps. Then, before I even thought to stop him, Desmond handed him the parchment envelope with the deeds in it. Longwalker began to read through the deeds and seemed quite pleased with the areas mentioned and the amount of land. He then unfolded a piece of paper I had not noticed before. As he began reading it, I knew something was wrong. His eyes gave him away. He then asked about Lieutenant O'Shea again, and to his whereabouts. I explained once more, that he had been called away to Ft Rend. The tall Cherokee stood up and began walking towards the lodge door where his rifle stood against the wall. He began speaking quickly in Cherokee to his braves, who all stopped what they were doing. Longwalker had reached his gun and asked "Then why is his payroll sheet and orders still with you?" He waved the paper at me… just as I shot him!

My men quickly drew their pistols and made short order of killing the rest of the Indians. For a brief instant, we just stood there, then I began to gather up the map cases and Desmond grabbed the gold and deeds and through them in the box. Moore and Upshaw brought the horses around just as a hail of bullets and arrows rained down on us. Seems there were more Indians than we had known! I was struck in the side by a bullet and Desmond took an arrow to the right shoulder! I managed to mount my horse and was again struck, this time by an arrow to the leg! Our pack horse with the provisions was struck and went down! The only way out was a trail directly in front of us, and I yelled for the men to follow me! It was moonless night and the thick canopy of trees made it impossible to tell which way were headed, but it was the only way out!

After what seemed like an eternity of starless flight, we entered a small clearing where we were able to stop and assess our wounds. Desmond's wound was in his shoulder and from an arrow, which had broken off. Upshaw was able to push the remainder on through and then bandage it. I, on the other hand, was not so fortunate. The arrow in my leg had also broken off by now, but the remainder was lodged deep into the bone. It would have to be dug out later. The bullet in my side had gone completely through, but from the dark color of the blood, I knew it had hit a vital organ. It would most likely be terminal without immediate care. The loss of blood and the pain had made me nauseous and weakened me quickly, but I knew we had no time to rest. We found a game trail and headed what I hoped was southeast, searching for someplace to hide and rest. I sent Moore back on foot to erase as much of our trail as possible.

The professor stood watching me as I finished reading this part of the journal.

"Mr Hawkes, you do understand that most of this part of the journal was written after the Sergeant was wounded? It is mostly scribbles that we had to interpret. Some, if not all, of the last parts are written in blood, but he bore down hard enough to inscribe it into the pages and we were able to make out most of it. So, what do you think of our Sergeant now?"

I looked at the remaining pages of the journal yet to be read.

"Well, sir, this is definitely confirmation that the maps did exist. And it seems likely that we now know why Sergeant Combs didn't make it, but what of the other men? Did one of them perhaps go on to finish the mission, or could the maps still be buried somewhere in that canyon?"

"No, young man, I don't think the mission was ever completed. I have the advantage of having completed the journal. Most all of the last pages are in blood and have faded badly and some of it is pure speculation on our part. But before you continue on, lets' explore the ramifications of what we have read so far. Primarily, the mention of deeds and titles to land being bequeathed to the Cherokee. Those could be of much more historical value than any collection of old maps! If these deeds were ever discovered, there is no telling what type of controversy they might ignite! If there was any legitimacy to them, who now might own these lands and who has rightful claim to them? It astounds the imagination as to what might become of them!"

"My God, Professor! I hadn't thought at all about that! I was just thinking of what a historical find the maps and gold would be!"

As I said this, the part of my brain that harbors my lawyer's education began to kick in, especially in regards to the reservation.

"But Professor, the deeds and acreage that encompass the reservation today, might they have been part of this original agreement?"

"Well, Mr Hawkes, I really doubt it. I'm sure you recall the history surrounding William Thomas and his purchase of thousands of acres of land with Cherokee money, and how a charter was formed that allowed the Cherokee to own land as a corporation, and not individually. But we will definitely have to research it. I see a very interesting story here, especially if they are ever recovered! No telling what states the acreage is in, or what has been built on them in the last 150 years! And it does present a fine bit of pondering! Continue on reading young man, for it gets even more interesting in the upcoming pages!"

◆◆◆◆◆

I began to read the next entry in the journal. There was no date on this page, and while it appeared to still be in ink, the handwriting was rapidly deteriorating.

The next thing I recall is Desmond helping me down from my horse. They had tied me to the saddle so I would not fall completely off. Desmond had found a small cave where we could rest and tend to our wounds. The amount of blood covering my saddle confirmed what my body was telling me, that I am gravely wounded and can not precede any further without some rest and attention given to my wounds. Desmond helped me into the cave and cleared a spot for me, spreading out my bedroll and his. He then began collecting small dry twigs and branches, hoping to start a small smokeless fire after sundown. He knew as well as I, that if we did not get these wounds tended to soon, infection would set in. Moore stepped into the cave and said he had found a small creek and was taking all of the canteens to fill them. After that, I once again succumbed to the pain and passed out.

When I next awoke, Desmond was tending to the wound in my side, and had already removed the piece of arrow from my leg and bandaged it. I thanked God for the fact that I had remained unconscious during the painful procedure. Desmond has a small fire going and a cup of broth ready for my consumption.

While I sipped the broth, he gave me the rundown on both his and my injuries. Upshaw had tended to the wound in Desmond's shoulder and it was healing well, but the same could not be said for my leg or my side wound. He began to whisper in my ear, telling me that he had overheard Upshaw and Moore talking about the gold! He thought they might be planning to make off with it! They were just waiting to see if my wounds proved to be fatal! He was beginning to fear for his life, and mine, should they get tired of waiting! Between the pain and the fever, I passed out again, and when I came to the conversation with Desmond seemed to me like a bad dream. It was dark now, and Moore and Upshaw lay quietly asleep in their bedrolls while Desmond stood watch outside of the cave. I called to him as best I could, and he finally entered the cave, waking Upshaw to relieve his watch. He lie down close to me and handed me more broth. 'Do you remember our earlier conversation?' he asked me. I admitted that it was a bit vague, so he repeated his worries to me. He had also taken the liberty of reloading my pistols and showed me where he had placed them under my bedroll, 'just in case,' he said. I tried to remain awake to question him further, but once again succumbed to the pain and blacked out.

When next I awoke, I was able to sit up a bit and see the sun rising above the mountains. The constant attention to my wounds from Desmond, and the beef broth had given me some strength back. Enough to where I thought I might be able to ride soon. I asked Desmond how long had we been in this cave and was astonished to learn that we had been here for 5 days! As I sat up straighter, I felt the guns under my bedroll and recalled our earlier conversations. When Moore and Upshaw returned with several rabbits, we all agreed that we should move out come tomorrow morning. There had been no sign of the Cherokee, and Upshaw had scouted us a path down off the mountain we were on. My stomach full and wounds cleaned again, I drifted off to sleep to avoid the pain.

I had refilled my coffee cup and was just adding some creamer, when I heard someone walk into the break room. Just as I was turning around, a stunning redhead walked up and stuck her hand out, saying

"And you must be Mr. Hawkes. Carrie Trent, professor Hartshorne's associate."

I shook hands with her, noticing the calluses and close cut fingernails. And the tight fitting shorts. And the tight fitting t-shirt. And the amazing smile and bright green eyes! Once again, I was trying to talk with what seemed like an egg in my throat. *'I have got to learn to get over this'* I thought to myself.

"NNNice to meet you," I stammered.

"An amazing story and find, Mr. Hawkes! I've been discussing the historical significance of the maps with Andy, and he has asked me if I could finish my work in Africa in time to represent the University on this one. I'm sure old Andy Jack would love to go himself, but his age and health are becoming an issue anymore. What are your plans and what kind of time table are we talking about?"

"I really haven't thought that far ahead yet. We have to determine whose property the site is actually on, and as the legal counsel for the Reservation, I have to coordinate everything through Miss Yellow Wing at the Museum. Perhaps you have met her?" I asked.

"Oh, yes. Yellow Wing and I are quite acquainted. We worked together as grad students some 6 or 7 years ago. She is quite the dedicated student of Cherokee history. I tried to get her to come and work for me several times in Europe and Africa, but she seems quite happy to remain right here. It would be nice to work with her on this project."

I stared into those amazing green eyes and knew that I had better confer with Yellow Wing before making any promises to Ms. Trent. It would be difficult to say no to her. "Well, it was really nice meeting you. I need to get back and finish reading the journal. We are going to the site next week to do a GPS reading and determine the boundaries regarding the location," I said, trying to sound professional. "I will pass along your hellos to Yellow Wing when next I see her."

Ms. Carrie Trent smiled at Deuce with a smile that would melt butter. "You do that. I'm sure she'll be thrilled to know I am back."

Somehow, Deuce didn't think so.

Now armed with a fresh cup of coffee, I went back to the classroom we were using for the journal's presentation. The next pages contained fewer sentences of the Sergeant's, with the interpretations typed below the actual writings. The Professor had warned me that they might not be verbatim, and some guessing had been required. He had warned me that nearly all of the final entries were done in what they had assumed was blood. A lab test had confirmed his assumptions. This made the last entries even more haunting as the journal concluded.

My leg wound is getting steadily worse. I fear that if we do reach a doctor, his only course will be amputation! I have no idea where we are, as Desmond has been leading my horse with me tied on once again. The terrain has become much more difficult to traverse, and the trail has all but disappeared, though Upshaw swears this is the way. Moore has discovered another secluded cave hidden amongst the brush. It is here we will stop and rest for a day or 2. Desmond helped me dismount and set me up inside the cave while he went to explore the surrounding area. He returned shortly, got a fire going, and made me as comfortable as possible. While he was arranging our gear, he told me of another exit, one that opened up into a box canyon. You have to go around a bend in the rear of the cave to see it, so he suggests we not mention it to the others. He then lays his bedroll near mine, hides his extra pistol beneath the blanket, as well as placing mine near me. Moore then entered, and I asked him to take first watch while Upshaw goes to hunt small game for our supper. He throws me a salute and he and Upshaw go about their business. Once they had gone, Desmond repeated his worries to me, and vowed to remain by my side no matter what. I thanked him profusely, and they were the last words ever spoken between us!

The next time I awakened was to the loud words of argument, and then gunfire! I sat up as quickly as I could and used my newly cut crutch to rise up and hobble to the entrance. I was shocked to see Desmond lying there dead, and Moore loading the gold and the last of the provisions on his horse. I pointed my pistol at them and demanded they drop their weapons. Moore spun around as Upshaw went for his rifle! I shot him twice through the heart just as Moore fired, striking me in the lower abdomen, and causing me to spin on my crutch and thereby avoiding his second shot! I emptied my pistol, hitting Moore in the face, but also hitting his horse and they both fell to the ground dead! Fortunately, the gold was on the up side of the horse, as well as the maps. But the remaining provisions were now under 1200 pounds of horse, and I doubted I had the strength to move it. And with this latest wound, I also doubted that I would need them!

I turned my attention to Desmond. That he was dead was obvious, shot once in the head and once in the chest. That he had died for me instead of joining them and leaving me to die, actually hurt worse than my wounds! I knew I must find someway to bury him. I would leave the others for the buzzards! My newest wound had yet to start aching, and I knew I was most likely suffering from shock. I needed to take care of him before the pain set in. I drug the gold and maps into the cave, as well as all of the canteens and what few provisions I could scrounge from the other horses. I then used Desmond's horse to drag him into and through the cave, and into the canyon he had found. What a beautiful canopied enclosure! I knew this would be a fine resting place for him, and most likely me too.

Hobbling around on my crutch, I discovered a sheer granite rock face that had an opening at the bottom about 8 feet long and 2 feet from the ground to the edge of the rock. I don't remember much now, but I somehow managed to roll Desmond into the opening then cover it with rock and dirt.

All I could think about afterwards was where to hide the maps and gold. The gold wasn't important, but the maps must not be found. I laid them in front of Desmond's grave and went back through the cave to the bodies outside. While I had no intention of burying the traitorous scum, I did need to move the bodies away from the cave, as they were likely to attract a bear or cougar. I again somehow managed to tie their feet with a rope and have the horses drag them to a clearing, then stripped the horses and set them free. I then sat down to rest. It was there that I awoke shivering and feverish. How I made it back to the cave..I don't know..I remember talking to Desmond and him telling me that I was going to die if I didn't get a fire going and tend to my wounds. I remember him helping me sit up, start the fire and warn me that they were going to bushwhack us.....

After reading the last few sentences, Deuce sat back and scratched his head. They didn't seem so ominous typed on the paper, but when he looked up at the white board and seen the fractured scribbling that was done in blood, a cold chill ran down his back. He realized the poor Sergeant had been hallucinating. How he had managed to accomplish his labors while so severely injured was a testament to his strength and character. Deuce looked at the remaining pages with the few blood scrawled sentences on each page. Had they been written in the same script as the rest, there would have been 1 more page instead of six. He finished the last swallow of his now cold coffee and picked up the last page, noticing all of the question marks and guess work.

When I woke this time, it all seemed like a bad nightmare. Then the pain and the realization that it wasn't, well, that was even worse. I ache so bad in so many places. I know I won't survive long. I spot the maps and gold and know I must hide them somewhere. I exit the cave and walk some distance. I scratch the distance on a gold coin. I turn toward the rising sun and walk again, scratching the amount of steps on another coin. I repeat this until I find two places to conceal the maps. Done, maps are hidden..now for the gold..

I lay here in this cave, using my last life's blood for ink to write this I write this hoping someday someone will find my journal ...I bury it here next to me ...my decision made. And I deem this mission a success. I will now surely die in this cave unless I can summon the strength to move once more...I have found the perfect place to die. I'm not going to die slowly and painfully. I will now hide this document case ...hope that someday history will know that I, Sgt. Burton L Combs did complete his mission ...I place this cross on this tree to mark my final resting place ...May my wife forgive me for leaving her alone. May God forgive me for what I am about to do...

CHAPTER 10

THE SEARCH BEGINS

W HILE DEUCE WAS reading the final pages of the journal, the professor and his team had finished examining the skull he had brought in. It was now obvious as to what the sergeant had been asking God's forgiveness for. The hole in the skull was undoubtedly from a bullet, and easily reasoned to be self inflicted. And after several washings in a solution that the professor claimed was a secret recipe, the gun barrel parts had been cleaned enough to determine that it was indeed etched in silver and gold. But it was pure guesswork to say that it had been Lieutenant O'Shea's.

Professor Hartshorne came over to the table where Deuce and Dr. Trent sat eating lunch. He carried in his hands several documents.

"Mr. Hawkes, Carrie, may I join you for a moment? I have the latest information on the characters that were accompanying our Sgt. Combs.."

"By all means, Andy, please join us," replied Dr. Trent. "I can't wait to find out more about these men! I think this is going to be a very interesting dig, if we can talk Deuce into letting us join him!"

'Well, I also have some paperwork with a few suggestions on that matter. But I'll leave that to you, Carrie, and see if you can persuade him to include us in whatever he and Yellow Wing decide to do. But let me read these new findings to you first. It seems our Sergeant and his companions were all listed as missing in action in some records we discovered through the South Carolina Historical Society. They seem to be the only ones who have any records regarding the Militia. When the Union sacked Charleston, the building housing all of the payroll records and enlistment information was burned to the ground. Some historians believe it was intentionally set afire to keep the Union from knowing the names of all of the soldiers and them being tried for treasonous acts, or some other retribution. But we have come across a few documents that actually list them as deserters. Wouldn't it be nice to present Sgt. Comb's journal to their families and erase the stigmata of desertion from their family records? To let them know that they died honorably while on a secret mission?"

"Well, Professor, while that would be nice for some of them, the whole story would have to come out, and Moore and Upshaw's families may not want to know the truth of their character. His journal makes them out to be bushwhackers and thieves!"

"I hadn't really thought about that part, but I suppose you're right. Yes, I see where that could raise a problem, as we only have one man's word on that. Your legal mind at work, Mr Hawkes? But at some point, the whole story is going to come out and I would like to try and rectify the wrong and shame the stigma of desertion that may have haunted their families for generations! It would only be right to try and clear their names!"

"Yes, sir, I understand and definitely agree. Lets' just see where this information leads us first. There may be much more we can discover to prove the journal oneway or another."

The professor looked Deuce in the eye, and said, "Deuce, you do know that I can't actually head up this expedition myself? To old and frail for fieldwork anymore, I'm afraid. Oh, I can run up and down these air conditioned hallways like a fireball, only because I disappear for a nap or 2 and take my medications on time! But my associate here is more than qualified and will be available soon, won't you, my dear? And it being so close to home for her, it would almost be like a vacation!"

"To be honest, sir, we had already briefly discussed that very issue. I think Dr. Trent was just waiting on you to officially ask her. She and I were just talking about a joint venture to include the reservation and the University."

"Marvelous, just marvelous! I knew you 2 would get along splendidly! I have an idea. Carrie, why don't you look over these papers that I took the liberty of having drawn up, and see if they meet your approval as far as the expenditures and personnel go. You may take as many of my grad students as you deem fit. And Mr. Hawkes, you also examine the paperwork and see if you think Ms. Yellow Wing would agree, and you can both do this tonight at the Whitney House Restaurant at Lake Sevier, where I keep a table reserved. How does that sound?" asked the professor.

Before I could say anything, Dr. Trent jumped up and hugged the professor's neck. "Why, thank you Andy Jack! And I know this is considered a business expense, right? So bring you the receipt?"

"Yes, yes, dear, bring me the receipt. And try not to indulge in too much expensive champagne! Well, you kids have a good time. I'm afraid I actually have business to conduct and go to work for a bit. Good day!"

And with that, he turned and took off before I could thank him…. or refuse him.

After the gracious invitation from the professor, I went to my apartment and cleaned up.

I picked out one of my regular workday suits and laid it on the bed. While I was drying my hair, I decided that since I'm on vacation, no suits! Instead, I chose a nice collared pullover and some slacks, but pocketed a tie just in case it was house policy at the restaurant. Some places are still like that. I then called Yellow Wing and told her about the offer from Professor Hartshorne, with the University to pick up half of the expenses.

"And who is he going to send in his place?" she asked. "I know he is getting to old to do field work. It wouldn't happen to be a Miss Trent, would it?"

"Uh, yeah. In fact, I'm having dinner with her tonight to go over the legalities involved. Of course, it all depends on the GPS co-ordinates and whose property the site is actually on."

"Hmm. I see. Well, you have a good time. But let me warn you about Carrie Trent. She is a very motivated and a career driven, manipulative bi..uhh.. woman. Do not sign or agree to anything until we get the exact location and I have a chance to go over it with you! I know you are a big time lawyer and all. But when it comes to archaeology and the expenses and who has possession and rights at a dig site, you are clueless!"

"Uhhh, yes mam. I hadn't planned on signing anything without your approval. It is only a casual dinner invitation from the professor and Dr. Trent, just to discuss the basics. I take it you know each other well?" I asked, realizing that there are times when I need to learn to keep my mouth shut.

"We worked at a few dig sites together. We both went to UT and worked under Professor Hartshorne in Africa and Asia. I had already decided that my goal was to come back to the reservation and concentrate on Cherokee history and do historical digs around here and create scenes for the museum. Her goal is to be a world renowned archaeologist, and she will do anything to anybody to achieve her goal!"

"Okay…I'll sure remember that. I'll be sure to get copies of everything for you to look at. Would you care to join us?" I asked, and knew as soon as I said it, open mouth, insert foot!

"Oh no, you go ahead and have a good time with your new friend. Just remember to tip well. The only Cherokee usually allowed in that establishment are just the wait staff." And with that she hung up.

CHAPTER 11

THE DEVIL IS IN THE PLANNING

B EN HACKETT HAD thought he was one of Professor Hartshorne's most reliable interns and student for sometime. There wasn't anything he wouldn't do for the old man. He was the proverbial brown noser, but after 2 years of sucking up to the old geezer he still hadn't gotten the respect or assignments he thought he deserved. And with this new discovery close to home, he had once again been passed over because that pet bitch of his had come home for a holiday! Letting her take the lead and he again being assigned to more menial tasks!

It was while he was cleaning the old skull, that he had heard the professor and that Indian lawyer discussing the maps, and then something about land deeds and titles, treaties and litigation. After that, every time the lawyer showed up, he found some reason to remain close by and listen in on their conversations. When he finally heard the full story, about what an uproar of legalities these documents could cause if found, he knew he had to be included in the team going to the dig site. The documents could very well be worth a lot of money to the right people. And the first one he thought of, was his Dad's friend, Rayford S. Trowbridge, the billionaire owner of Trowbridge Forest Products. It just so happened that he owned thousands of acres bordering the reservation and 2 different National parks. If these deeds included land he now owned, they could get tied up in court for years, preventing him from harvesting the lumber, costing him millions in litigation, too! He would call his Dad and have him set up a meeting with Mr. Trowbridge!

And he was going to need a partner. Preferably someone from the reservation dig crew. And he thought he knew just the one, Ronnie Cloud, Ms. Yellow Wing's assistant. He wouldn't ever think about volunteering to harm the reservation, but Ben knew something about old Ronnie that very few did. Being bi-sexual himself, he frequented the gay clubs around Knoxville and Johnston City, and the hot spots around Fort Loudon Lake. It was while he was at the lake that he had seen Ronnie and another young man together. He had actually been surprised, for Ronnie was a big good looking guy with the traditional long braided hair. Real macho looking type, and it seemed he went out of his way to keep his secret. But first, he had to find out what it was worth to Mr. Trowbridge to keep these documents from ever seeing the light of day!

Ben's dad called him back within the hour and told him that Ray would meet him at the yacht club tomorrow evening at 6:30, then told him, "Son, dress nice and don't be late. All I told him was what you told me, that you had some information about possibly thousands of acres of timber rights that he might lose to the Cherokee. Now, I don't know what the hell you come across, but if it ain't legit and you make of fool me or yourself around Ray, don't you ever ask me for no more favors, you hear me?" And then he hung up. Ben and his dad hadn't gotten along well in years. Not since the time he had found out that Ben was gay by walking in on him and his partner at their lake cabin. Yeah, that had been a hell of a day!

Ben sat at the bar in the yacht club, nursing his third drink. He was dressed about as well as any Miami Vice aficionado would be. It was already a quarter til 7, and he had been there since 6 p.m. He was just about to order his 4th drink when he heard a deep voice say loudly, "You must be Ben Junior!"

Ben turned around to see a white haired gentleman about 6'3" tall, immaculately dressed dressed in a 5000 dollar Armani blue and silver suit. His smile and bright blue eyes denied his true age of 66 years, and he could have passed for, and was, the epitome of what a wealthy grandfather should look like. Ben stood up from his seat to shake hands with him.

Trowbridge said, "Come on, I have a booth in back that is permanently reserved for me. It'll be more private."

Ben followed him to the booth section at the back of the club, a little wobbly at first, not knowing if it was the alcohol or his nerves making him shaky. After they were seated, Trowbridge ordered a round of drinks, then said, "Well, it's your show son, so get with it. What the hell could those Indians do that would cost me thousands of acres and millions of dollars?"

Ben took a long drink from his Jack and coke and began telling him the whole story. When he was through, Trowbridge just sat there and stared at him. Ben noticed that the smiling blue grandfather eyes had now turned to more of a blue steel in nature, and reminded Ben of the cold dead eyes of a shark. He finished his drink and sat there waiting for Trowbridge to say something, anything, instead of just staring at him with those cold blue eyes.

"Son, this had better not be some kind of scam you're trying to pull, because if it is, I'll drop you in one of my tree chippers and you'll wind up plant food. Now, if this is true, well, you should have some kind of proof for me, right?"

"Yes sir! Hell, I nearly forgot!" Ben reached inside of his jacket and pulled out the copies he had made of the journal. It had been the last menial task required by the Professor, to run 20 copies of all of the notes and journal pages for the old goat's assistants to use for research on the individuals listed.

Trowbridge ordered more drinks and began to peruse the notes. When he finished, he turned to Ben and asked, "Just what did you have in mind, son? How are you going to help me, and just what do you want for it? How much and what do I get for my money?"

Ben looked him in the eye, his courage emboldened by the whiskey, and said, "I was thinking 20,000 dollars. To make sure the documents never see the light of day if found.

I'm going to need some help, and I think I have found the right guy." Ben went on to explain his reasoning and ideas about recruiting Ronnie Cloud.

"Well, okay. We could invite to come right here. Now how much is his assistance going to cost me? Damn sure not paying him another 20 grand! Tell you what, you pay him out of your 20, and we have a deal. But if the documents are found, I want them brought to me. I want to see them for myself. No documents, no money!"

"Yes sir. And I was only going to offer him 5000 dollars and a promise to keep his secret quiet. I'll try to arrange a meeting with him in a week or so. I'll call and let you know when. If you would call here and advise the bartender that I'll be using your booth, and leave a check for the 5 grand with him, you need not even show up, sir."

Trowbridge stood up and looked down at Ben. He then stuck out his hand and said, "Ok, young man, we have a deal. Call me and let me know what day and time. I'll be here, too, but don't speak to me unless I come over. And have another drink on me if you'd like. I'm going to go read through all of this again, then talk to my lawyer and have him do some research and see if there is any history archived somewhere to validate these claims. Good night."

"Goodnight sir."

Ben took him up on his offer of another drink. In fact, he had several more as he schemed out his plan. With any luck, it would be him or Ronnie who found the case with the deeds and documents. If someone else found them first, well, the documents would just have to go missing. And once he had them, the 20,000 dollars was just the down payment......

CHAPTER 12

A JOINT VENTURE

R ED AND I sat at the bar in Harrah's Casino, discussing some of the legal ramifications involved in the joint venture between the EBCI and the UT archeology department. He and I had flown over the canyon and cave site using my GPS co-ordinates collected from my cell phone. According to the grid plats furnished by the Department of Interior, the cave and canyon were actually on a dividing line that placed the first half of the location on the reservation, which included the cave. The remainder of the site was on National Forestry property, which included the tree with the bayonets in it. This discovery had led to the conference, which was to take place in a couple of hours here at Harrah's.

Dr. Carrie Trent and her dig team were here representing the university and meeting with Yellow Wing and her team from the reservation. A team that she had hastily assembled and included Red and I. Since my lavish dinner with Dr. Trent, Yellow Wing and I had researched hundreds of tribal documents going back 150 years. We found only one mention of the supposed deal between the Union and the Cherokee, and only one record mentioning the betrayal by the Union and theft of the maps, and murder of 12 Cherokee braves. According to the letter, the Union denied any wrong doing, then accused the Cherokee of ambushing Lieutenant O'Shea and the couriers and stealing the gold and land deeds, nullifying any promise of giving said lands back to the Indians. According to the same letter in the records, as all of the fingers were being pointed at each other, the bodies of the Lieutenant and his entourage were discovered buried along creek bed 10 miles from the rendezvous site, that being where the 12 Cherokee were found dead. But who had done what was still a mystery. Unfortunately, right as the investigation began, a conflict known as the Civil War erupted and took precedence over the situation. All individuals involved in the investigation were re-assigned to more urgent matters.

Now armed with our newest information, Red and I were ready to call the meeting to order.

"Good evening all," Red said into the microphone. "For those of you who don't know me, my name is Rudy Croixe, or just 'Red' to most everybody around here. I am the tribal liaison with Harrah's for the EBCI, and a member of the Tribal Council and will speak for the EBCI on all manners concerning our involvement in this joint venture. Standing next to me is my cousin, Deuce Hawkes, who by now most of you know is the one who discovered the burial site while out deer hunting. He is also the legal representative for the EBCI from Bruce, Fenton, and Hawkes law firm in Knoxville. His Grandfather also sits on our Tribal Council. So, with these introductions out of the way, I'll turn it over to him."

Deuce looked out at the assembled crowd and cast of characters, recognizing most. They were seated like to opposing armies, with a virtual 'No Man's Land' of empty tables between them. It seemed his job was going to be to unite these 2 separate factions together for this historical event. He patted Red on the shoulder, excusing him, and basically repeated what his cousin had said. The only difference being that he added the information that the permits had been requisitioned for both parties to investigate the site as an historical find. The objective was to determine exactly what the South Carolina Militia had clandestinely been doing in the area previous to the war, and their involvement in the Cherokee's mapping of the mountain pathways. The discovery of Sgt. Combs' journal had led to the confirmation of the Union's involvement, and answered the question as to why the Cherokee were at odds with the Union at the start of the Civil War, preferring to side with the Confederates.

Deuce paused long enough to take a drink and scan the audience again.

"Miss Yellow Wing and I have discovered more information pertaining to the mission being operated out of Ft. Rend by the Union in 1859 and 60.

There was mention of land being offered, as well as payment in gold, for the Cherokee's participation. If these documents are discovered, the historical ramifications could be very unique, especially since we now know what happened, due to Sgt. Combs' blood soaked journal. Professor Hartshorne's research team has been invaluable in their pursuit of information regarding the different characters involved in this scenario, and with their team and ours, I think we can achieve the goal of making this a very historical and even legendary find! Now, if I could get the Professor and Dr. Trent to join Red, Yellow Wing, and I, we can go over the paper work and arrangements, as well as the division of costs and labor. And once again, thank you all for your participation."

Deuce watched Yellow Wing and Dr. Trent both approach him in the 'No Man's Land' of tables from different directions. He imagined it to be like watching a Jaguar and a Puma both approaching the same carcass, only instead of a deer, he was the game.

Ben sat at the table with Mike Lowery and Jonah White, helping himself to the free drinks and buffet being provided by the EBCI. The Professor and Carrie Trent, along with her personal assistant, Jeanie Stiles, sat at their table reserved only for UT's high and mighty, not letting those without a doctorate join them. That was all right though, for he had been busy watching Ronnie Cloud since he had entered and was just waiting for the right time to deliver his message and invitation. His main hope was the Ronnie's sexual proclivities and curiosity would cause him to accept the invitation. There was also the slight hint as to money in the note, hoping that if the sexual connotations didn't entice him, dollar signs would.

Finally, Ben saw his chance and followed him into the Men's room. When Ben entered, he noticed that Ronnie had chosen a stall at the far end of the restroom. There was only one other person in the room, and as soon as he left, Ben walked by the stall and hurriedly slid an envelope under the door and exited the restroom. He then joined Dr. Trent at her table and became involved in the conversation about what he could do to help on the upcoming project.

Ronnie had only been seated in the stall for a few minutes, when a pair of brown leather shoes had paused by the door just long enough to cause him to stash the little mirror and straw he had just sat on his knee. Then all of a sudden, an envelope had slid under the door, coming to rest against his moccasin. He reached down and picked up the envelope, both curious and scared as to what might be inside. Ronnie was an individual of many secrets, and he was quickly worried as to which ones might have been discovered. As he read the note, it became clear that several had been found out!

Mr. Cloud,

I have not had the opportunity to introduce myself as yet, but I have been informed that I will be working with you in the near future. I thought we might get together for a few drinks this week and discuss a joint venture that could be profitable to us both. And it seems we have a few things in common, as I too, have been to McKenna's Landing on many occasions and have witnessed you there also. Such lovely cabins, and so private, aren't they? But let's keep these little secrets between us, shall we? Enclosed you will find a guest card granting you access to the lower bar at the Southern Tennessee Yacht Club at Sevier Resevoir. Please meet me there at 8:00 pm Tuesday. I think you will find my invitation rewarding. See you then. Oh, and do be careful not to break your little mirror...7 years bad luck, you know?

Ronnie sat there somewhat shell shocked. It seems that some of his secrets weren't so secret after all. The mirror comment, plus the mention of McKenna's Landing was very disturbing. The Landing was a private fish camp with dozens of secluded cabins, but was also an exclusive rendezvous spot for many of the areas gay community. Apparently not as private as he had thought! He examined the enclosed guest card and found no name on it but his, and just a boat slip number. He had never been there, but knew it was a refuge for the extremely rich. And he was quite certain that the only Indians to ever enter there were the wait staff or kitchen help!

Ronnie walked back into the banquet room and scanned the tables. Of the 25 or so people sitting in there, he couldn't even guess who might have delivered the note. By excluding the women, that reduced the number to 14. It couldn't be Red or Deuce, or it least he didn't think it was likely. That only left the men from the Forestry Department or the university, and without examining everyone's shoes, his only other choice was to show up Tuesday! As he was staring intently at the group, Yellow Wing approached him.

"Ronnie, are you okay?" she asked.

"Huh? Oh yeah, yeah, maybe a few too many gin and tonics, on top of all of that prime rib. Stomach fluttering a bit, you know?"

Yellow Wing just laughed and said, "Yes, I do know! You go on home if you need to. I'll bring the notes and records from the Tribal Council by tomorrow and you and I can go over them with Deuce. See you then."

"Okay, see you tomorrow."

Ben had watched Ronnie come into the room with that deer in the head lights look. He was doing his best to examine everyone in the room for some kind of recognition. Ben turned his back to him as he heard Yellow Wing talking. He was pretty sure it was going to be a restless night for one Mr. Cloud!

CHAPTER 13

TRIBAL RECORDS

EUCE SHOWED UP at Yellow Wing's office the next morning to examine some documents that she had discovered in the Tribal records. So far, they were the only recorded mention of the maps and any deal with the Union in 1859. The numerous inquiries that he and Yellow Wing had made to all of the different historical societies had all come up negative, no idea what they were talking about was the most common answer.

All Grandfather could come up with were rumors and myths. He said there might be some old transcripts from the early days of the reservation that Yellow Wing had yet to catalog, so she had been searching for days and finally had something interesting to show him.

"What I have here is a collection of treaty violations compiled from my research. Not only Cherokee, but Shoshone, Cree, Choctaw, Seminole, and many more tribes out west. But there is no mention of maps or any land ever being offered for services rendered by the Cherokee. But, I did find one mention of the maps written by your Grandfather's great uncle. "He- who- moves- like- the- wind" is a fair interpretation of his name in English. Here, read this while I go get us some coffee."

I sat down at one of the tables and turned the lamp on. The letters were all written in Cherokee, but she had provided pages of interpretations. I tried to imagine what it was like around here 150 years ago. The letters were written in 1870. I guess that he got older, he felt the need to chronicle his memoirs, to preserve his brother's memory and pass on a piece of history that for some reason had failed to be recorded by anyone else. The information he provided was the second side of a many faceted story. As Yellow Wing returned with the coffee, I began to read my ancestor's letter.

'In the white man's month of March, in his year of 1859, my brother, Long Walker, and myself went to meet the big redhaired man known as Lieutenant O'Shea. He made us an offer of lands and gold coin for help with mapping the mountains through our ancestoral lands and several other mountain ranges we were familiar with. He said that there might be a war between the white men of the south, called see-sess-shun-ist, and the white men of the northern union. I told him that his white man's war should not include us, as we did not really care who won. Maybe you can kill each other off and we can get back all of our lands. O'Shea just laughed and said there were way too many white men for that to ever happen. But then he said that for every Cherokee that helped his map makers, they would receive 100 dollars in gold coin, and give the tribe many square miles of land. I did not know what a square mile was, and Long Walker made him circle the lands on a map. It did not seem like a very big circle to me. He explained that they wanted to move men and supplies secretly through the mountain trails and passes that were only known by the Indians and very few white men. Made sense to me. We had been doing it to them for many generations. Long Walker told him it would take many moons to map all of the trails. How many Cherokee did he want?

And did the great white chief have that much gold? O'Shea laughed again and said that he had more men than trees in the forest, and enough gold to fill all of the lodges ten times over. At that time, I thought he was lying. I know better now.

Mt brother told him we must present this to the council, and we needed to see something on paper to show the council about the land. He said he would bring us the papers called deeds and titles. We knew what deeds and titles were. The same papers that allowed them to take our lands in the first place! He also said that we were not the only tribe he could talk to, and would it not be a shame if some other tribe got our lands?"

"Well, what do you think so far?" asked Yellow Wing, as she sat down beside me with a fresh cup of coffee. The aroma of coffee mixed with the jasmine and cinnamon of her hair had me thinking about anything but old Indian lore. With her sitting so close, I would never be able to finish reading it all.

"I think we need to investigate this Lieutenant O'Shea some more and see if there are any records of his involvement with the Cherokee. Maybe find out what unit he was with, or what they claimed happened to him and why. Might try to track down some of his relations and see what kind of story they were given as to the cause of his demise."

"That sounds like a good idea," she said, and left to go see what she could dig up on the computer. I continued reading my ancestor's letter.

"We met with Lt. O'Shea on the 1st day of their month of April and told him of the Council's decision. The Elders had agreed to help the Union with the maps, but that was all. We would not send Cherokee braves to fight in the event there was a war. He said that was fine, that the maps were more important. He said his chief would be sending 16 mapmakers, and would need 16 Cherokee to guide them. He agreed to meet us in 10 days. Two days later, I was thrown from a horse that was startled by a rattler and broke my leg. This was the reason why I didn't go to guide one of the mapmakers. It is also the reason I am not dead like my brother Long Walker.

"It had taken our braves over 6 moons to make all of the maps. Some of them had not seen their families since they left. We met with Lt. O'Shea and let him examine the maps the men made. He said he would take them and show them to his chief and then bring us our gold and deeds. Long Walker said no. He would take one map to show his chief, then they would meet us at the southern hunting lodge with the gold and deeds, and there he would surrender the maps to him. A date was set for sometime in September. I did not go. I was busy with other things and do not know what happened. Some of our braves returned saying they had been a few miles from the lodge when they had heard much gunfire, and by the time they arrived, the bluecoats had fled and all of the Cherokee were dead! They tried to track their trail, but it got dark and they lost them. We went back to retrieve our dead, and the next morning tried again to pick up their trail. They were as good as us, and we never found them. This I have written, this is all that I know of my brother's death. April 7, 1870.

CHAPTER 14

THE ALLIANCE

R ONNIE CLOUD SAT in the private club waiting to see who had invited him here. The club was one of the Souths best kept secrets, located on a private lake that connected to Sevier Resevoir. It could be accessed by car from a private road, or from the water via a private canal. It was constructed to resemble an old antebellum mansion, and the restaurant could only be entered by club members or their guests, with the appropriate invitation. But the lower bar was for club members only, and any guest had to be accompanied by a member. Or so the sign said. Ronnie had checked the boat slip earlier to see if there might be a name on it. There was no name, but there was a 60 foot yacht moored there. And when Ronnie entered the bar, he was immediately asked for his ID, then shown directly to a reserved table, which proved that whoever it was had enough clout to get Ronnie admitted alone!

The note he had received was serious enough that he had no choice but to come. The mention of a profitable endeavor had been enough to get his attention, but the mention of the Landing had sealed the deal. As he was thinking it over, a tall, handsome, blonde gentleman entered the bar and walked straight toward him.

"Mr. Cloud, I'm Ben Hackett, Dr. Trent's associate from UT." He stuck his hand out and Ronnie hesitantly shook it. He had recognized him instantly.

"I'm sure you have many questions as to why you were invited here, and I'll be happy to answer them all, but first, lets have a drink or 2 and order something to eat, shall we?

• • ◆ ◆ ◆ ◆ •

Ronnie wiped the prime rib juice from his mouth, finished his drink and laid the linen napkin on the table. He watched as Ben finished his Lobster Bisque, his curiosity eating at him the same way he had eaten his steak. Ben had been taking his time, enjoying the anxiety building up in Ronnie's eyes.

"So, Ronnie, have you heard anything about some supposed land deeds and titles that were promised to the Cherokee in 1859 or thereabouts? As Yellow Wing's #1 assistant, I'm sure you get to hear the inside scoop between her and Deuce?"

Ronnie stared at Ben for a moment, then answered, "Yeah, but probably no more than you have. Is that what this is all about? Because I can tell you that Deuce and her have been researching that for weeks, and so far have been unable to get any kind of confirmation from any government source that such a deal was ever proffered. And only one mention in some old tribal records. Nothing concrete to validate the sergeant's journal."

"Well, be it as it may, I have a business offer for you," said Ben. "You team up with me during the excavation of the site, and we do our best to be the one's who discover the maps and deeds, if they do exist. Only difference being, if we do find the deeds, and deeds only, to hell with the maps and gold, we sell them to Rayford Trowbridge and his associates for a substantial reward."

Ronnie gave Ben a look of incredulity. "Really? How much of a reward?"

"I'm thinking it will be a negotiable sum of many thousands at least. He owns or has the rights to hundreds of thousands of acres of timberland bordering the National forest and the reservation. If the deeds are actually found, they could be the cause of many years of legal fees and denied access to the lumber, costing Mr. Trowbridge and his associates millions in litigation and loss of product. But lets keep our asking price between us until we have the deeds in hand. My main question for you now, is do you really think they exist, and are you willing to help me find them?"

Ronnie sat there stunned for a few minutes, his Cherokee soul in torment as he deduced the outcome of said deeds. Could there actually be thousands of acres possibly given back to his people? How many people would be displaced? How many houses and businesses were now on that land, and how many years of litigation and fees would it take to secure that land for the Cherokee? He knew Ben was right. If those deeds existed and were found, their validity would be argued in court for years.

As he sat there taking it all in, his inner soul began a battle of attrition. Should he agree to help Ben simply for the money, and lest he forget, keeping his personal life secret? Or follow his Indian heritage and try to help his people get back millions of dollars worth of real estate?

Ben ordered more drinks while Ronnie contemplated his dilemma. When the drinks arrived, they were accompanied by a tall, silver haired man, in a beige business suit. Ronnie could tell by the cut of the cloth that he was looking at a 5000 dollar Armani suit, and just his demeanor alone conveyed wealth.

"Good evening Ben. Mind if I join you?"

"Mr. Trowbridge! What a pleasant surprise! Please, sir, join us," invited Ben.

Ronnie didn't know if it was going to be pleasant, but he knew damn well it no surprise. It was obvious to him that Ben didn't have the wealth needed to obtain membership to such an exclusive club.

"And you must be Ronnie Cloud. Rayford Trowbridge here. I gather you have had a decent meal while our friend has been explaining the situation to you?"

"Nice to meet you, sir," answered Ronnie. "I take it you are the Trowbridge of Trowbridge Forest Industries?"

Mr Trowbridge smiled a smile that reminded Ronnie of the crocodiles at the Knoxville zoo, all teeth.

"Yes sir, that would be me. If you are willing to help locate these mysterious deeds, and make sure they are delivered to me, I'll make sure you are well compensated for your involvement. As I am sure Ben has explained, the possible years of litigation and fees, well, it would be best if they are simply never found. On the other hand, if you do find them and I research them and discover that they in no way infringe upon my holdings, you can turn them in for whatever historical value they may have."

Trowbridge reached inside of his jacket and pulled out 3 envelopes. He handed one to Ben, who pocketed it without opening it. Ben knew what was in the second envelope, a check for 5000 dollars made out to Ronnie Cloud, but the 3rd envelope had him baffled. He handed Ronnie his envelope, and Ronnie pulled the check out, the equivalent of 2 months salary at the museum. Ronnie took a long pull off of his drink, then asked, "And for this amount, I am expected to do what?"

"Just make sure that if the deeds are discovered, that they wind up in my hands first. Then we can discuss a finder's fee."

Ronnie placed the check back in the envelope and handed it to Mr. Trowbridge.

"I can't do that sir," he said. And the blank blue eyes that stared back at him were pure shark's eyes, cold and dead. Trowbridge reached for the third envelope and was about to hand it to Ronnie.

"At least not for this check, too easy to trace. How about cash instead?" Ronnie asked. The elderly gentleman once again went from reptile to someone's doting grandfather, as a smile crept across his face. He pocketed the third envelope again and said,

"I'm sure that can be arranged, if you'll give me a few minutes?"

Trowbridge scooted his chair back and went to the bar phone. 10 minutes later he returned with an envelope containing 50 one hundred dollar bills. He handed it to Ronnie and stuck his hand out.

"Then we have a deal, Mr Cloud?"

"Yes sir, that we do," answered Ronnie as he shook hands. Ben then handed him a business card with several phone numbers on it.

"I'll text or call you whenever Dr. Trent and the team are headed for the reservation. We'll make our plans as we go. Goodnight."

Ronnie slowly staggered his way back to his truck, wondering just what he had gotten himself into. One thing he did know, just where to spend part of his new wealth. He was already on the phone, seeing if he couldn't score a little pick-me-up to help soothe his conscience.

After Cloud had left, Ben couldn't help but ask Mr. Trowbridge, "Well, what do you think? Will he stay committed to the cause?"

"Oh, I do believe he will, Ben. One way or another." He then pulled out the 3rd envelope and extracted a dozen photos showing Ronnie and a handsome young blonde guy in various sexual positions.

"I had a little insurance in case he needed convincing. The blonde in the photos is also a private detective, as well as a low level coke dealer, and gay." Trowbridge stood up and slipped on his jacket, laughing to himself all the way to the car.

CHAPTER 15

THE TROUBLE WITH BEARS

AFTER SPENDING THE last few days in Yellow Wing's company, Deuce was about to admit that he was falling for her. Her constant presence at his Grandfather's lodge seemed to indicate that maybe she was happy to be around him, too. He decided to ask his Grandfather for a little more information and history on her, fill in the years he had been away, explain why one so beautiful wasn't already married. He knew she spoke to the old man as a confidant and was as close to him as were his own family.

"So, you wish me to indulge in Reservation gossip, like is done on reality soap tv?" asked the wizened old man. "Maybe you should go to the washeteria on Mondays, when the old women go. It has many TVs, a game room, and a bingo parlor, where inquisitive young bucks can learn much just by imitating a mushroom. And like the protein base in which mushrooms thrive best, you too, could be enriched by such nutritional earfuls." He then leaned back in his chair and was instantly asleep, or so it seemed.

For someone who claims to have difficulty in understanding the English language, his point was well put and naturally clear to me, that he wasn't going to indulge my curiosity. I guess it was up to me to just ask her whenever she arrived. I began to embolden myself with several breakfast Mai-Tais. As I was on my 3rd one, I noticed a blue Toyota Landcruiser pull up in front of the lodge. As I walked out onto the porch, Dr. Carrie Trent exited the jeep, long red ponytail bouncing in the sun as she skipped up the steps. She was wearing a blue sleeveless shirt, tied in a knot halfway up her torso, and leaving about 8 inches of muscular abs showing. A pair of well sculptured tan legs exited her khaki shorts, proving how much time she spent in hot outdoor climates.

"Good morning, Deuce! I was hoping to find you here. May I come in?"

"Sure, please do," I answered. I couldn't take my eyes off of her. I actually forgot what I was fixing to do. It also seemed that Grandfather's snoring had taken on a decisive chuckling noise, even though his eyes remained closed.

Carrie entered the room and sat down at the big table. "Do you feel up to a ride down south today? I had told the professor that I would try and catch you today and get a feel for the area and layout a plan for the equipment to bring. I know, I know, we had agreed that we would all do this starting Monday, but it is such a beautiful Saturday, that I couldn't resist a scenic drive! Whatcha think, wanna go?"

"Uh, well, yeah, sure, why not? Would you like something to cold eat, er drink? Or eat? A Mai-Tai, maybe?" Seemed I was having trouble forming sentences again. And there goes that chuckling snore, too.

"Sure, a Mai-Tai sounds good, even this early. In fact, let me get my gallon thermos and we can fill it up and take it with us. You said we could make it as far as the old cabins in a jeep, so I brought one!"

A few minutes later, Deuce was filling up the thermos, finishing making some turkey sandwiches and preparing to leave, when Grandfather raised up from his recliner.

"And where should I say you have gone, in case anyone inquires?" he asked, making that noise again.

Dr. Trent stood at the door, waiting on him and his answer.

"Uh, well, uh, just say I went on a business trip. Yeah, a business trip and will return…uh …later on."

"Uh-Huh, business trip…yep I got it, okay. Seems business is booming around here," and with that the old man went back to sleep.

Monday morning lived up to it's reputation. It was foggy, humid, and overcast as the 2 groups met at the museum. Deuce was doing his best to organize the expedition and get underway, but Yellow Wing wasn't talking to him and was determined to do things her way. Deuce couldn't believe how stubborn she was being. On the other hand, every time he turned around, Dr. Trent was right there making suggestions. He had finally had enough and jumped into his jeep, hooked up the horse trailer and drove off!

He was just starting south, when he heard the C.B. radio beep. "Lawyer 1, you got it on, come back?"

Deuce grabbed the mic, "Go ahead Red, whats up?"

"Seen you take off and everybody scrambling to catch up. You okay?"

"Rodger, Red. If they want to sit and argue about every little thing, fine by me, but I'm going to get this show started, 10-4?"

"Yeah, 10-4. I take it you regret your little Saturday drive now? I forgot to warn you about a few of Yellow Wing's personality traits. One is her stubbornness, and, well, she can get pretty possessive and jealous if she likes someone, copy?"

Deuce laughed at that. "10-4 on the stubborn. I should have stayed at the Lodge, copy?" "Rodger. Well, be careful cousin, and watch out for the wildlife. And the animals, too!" Deuce heard Red's laughter as he hung up his mic. He looked in the mirror and was happy to see the procession behind him. Maybe they would actually get something done today, after all!

Ronnie was checking the 4 wheelers to make sure they were fastened down tight, when Ben pulled up in a jeep. Sitting beside him was a stocky young lady with a multitude of tattoos.

"Hiya Ronnie," Ben said. "You ready for this dig? You haven't actually ever been on a real archaeological dig before, have you? It's a lot more complicated than just digging around in the dirt!"

Ronnie walked up to the jeep and shook hands with Ben, then the young lady. "Jemma Lang, meet Ronnie Cloud."

"Nice to meet you. No, I haven't ever been on a real dig before with you professional types, though I have helped Yellow Wing a few times on smaller digs. Heard that these large digs are more like real work, and the cataloging can get pretty tedious."

Ben and Jemma both laughed at that. "Yeah, that's one way too put it. And don't wear anything you wouldn't stomp in the mud. Hopefully there is water close by that we can use to wash off any artifacts that we find.

But you just stick with me, and I'll show how to string grid sections and bag and tag objects we find. So, we'll see you there?" "Right, see ya there."

Deuce was unloading the horses when the UT team arrived. They went straight to the site that Dr. Trent had laid out Saturday on her visit with Deuce. Seemed that everyone thought they had had a fling while gone, and Deuce had to admit that he thought they were going to. But Carrie wasn't as easy as he had hoped. Her mind was just as fine as her body, and she knew how to use both to get what she wanted. That's how she wound up with the best camping spot for her team!

Deuce led the parade of people and 4 wheelers from the cabins to the canyon. He and the old paint ran point as far as the vehicles could go. The 4 wheelers could actually make it to the copse of trees that had kept the canyon hidden from mankind for all of these years.

From that point on, it was either by horse or on foot. Dr. Trent told him not to worry, that they would get the 4 wheelers and equipment all the way to the cave. She and her team broke out the chainsaws and cut a path about 5 foot wide. After a couple of hours, they had a path allowing them mobile access all the way to the cave entrance. They then brought up the rest of the equipment and established a base camp about a mile from the canyon.

Deuce led everyone through the cave, stopping to show them where the markings were on the walls, and then gave everyone a tour of the canyon. Dr. Trent and part of her team began to mark off a grid pattern, using tent stakes and bright orange string. The rest were assigned the duties of preparing the campsite. By nightfall, they had the grid laid out from the cave entrance all the way to 20 feet past the 'Bayonet Tree', to the granite wall 20 feet behind the tree.

Each section was lettered A-J, and each grid numbered 1-15. Sections were then assigned to pairs of diggers, one from the museum and one from the university. Ronnie and Ben paired up immediately and were assigned to sections G through J, per Ben's request. These sections ran from the entrance of the cave to the exit, then along the granite cliff face on the east side of the canyon.

Jemma Lang volunteered to team up with Yellow Wing, and Carrie Trent asked Deuce to be her partner. He felt trapped between a rock and a hard place, and the look he got from Yellow Wing prompted him to ask

Jemma to be his partner. Jemma realized the situation and agreed, leaving Yellow Wing and Dr. Trent to choose from the remaining members, for there was no way those two were going to pair up! So, at the end of the second day, the gird was finished, the teams chosen, and the assignments scheduled. The real work would begin tomorrow.

Deuce was sitting by his fire when Yellow Wing approached him. She unfolded a camp chair she had brought and sat across from him. The firelight reflected off of her raven black hair, and gave her already radiant skin a glow of health and beauty. Deuce was mesmerized by her smile and twinkling eyes, when he realized she was speaking to him.

"Uh, do what? I'm sorry, I didn't hear you," he stammered.

"I said, do you think we should assign someone to watch the camp and horses at night, due to the wildlife that might be attracted by the food we cook?"

Deuce thought for a moment, then said, "I lectured everyone before we left about keeping everything sealed and putting all of the garbage in that big metal drum we brought. Even so, bears and raccoon can get awfully creative when it comes to opening things, but I think we'll be all right. And the horses will make plenty of racket if they smell a bear or a cougar."

She poked the fire with a stick, stirring up the flames. "And what about you, Deuce? What are you going to do after this little adventure is over? Go back to your corporate law jungle and hide out for another five years, or are we going to see you around more often? You know, Grandfather really misses having you around, and we all miss your mom since she passed. Grandfather may seem like an eternal being, but he is getting on up there in age and may not be around that much longer. He won't tell anybody his age, but tribal records put him at 84."

Deuce smiled at that, just trying to imagine what all that old man had seen in his 84 years. "I think Red and I are going to build a cabin somewhere close to here. I was also wondering if you'd like to help me as co-author on a book I'm thinking of writing, depending on what all we find out here. So, yeah, I'll be hanging around for awhile."

"Why Deuce Hawkes, that is a splendid idea, and of course I would love to help you! So you go from attorney to author overnight?"

"Why not? John Grisham did it. In fact, there are several action writers with legal backgrounds. But how many of them have Indian backgrounds, too?"

Yellow Wing laughed while folding up her chair. "Well, goodnight Mr. Author. Better get rested up because the real work starts tomorrow." And with that, he watched her walk away, wishing so badly that she had stayed.

The next morning, as soon as Deuce's horse crested the hill and headed towards the cave, she began to get skittish. The closer to the cave she got, the more she snorted and tried to turn. Deuce finally took the hint and turned her around, heading back to the top of the hill. The line of 4 wheelers was coming up behind him, so he waved them over, Dr. Trent pulling up first.

"What's the matter Deuce?" she asked.

"Don't know for sure, but my horse is acting pretty strange, which could mean there is a bear or cougar in the area of the cave."

"Well, why don't you leave your horse here and you can ride down with me and we'll take a look. We both have guns, so we can scare it off if need be."

Carrie and Deuce rode into the area they had cleared the day before, which allowed them full access right up to the cave entrance. While he was still entranced from the warmth of her body and smell of her hair, she bailed off of the 4 wheeler and was into the cave, flashlight in one hand, gun in the other, not allowing him to play the macho hero and go first. As Deuce rounded the curve in the cave, he heard Carrie exclaim, "Oh dammit, dammit, dammit, all that work ruined!"

Deuce was taken aback by all of the damage done. The worktables were up ended and most of the grid work was now a tangled mess! There were bear tracks everywhere, and several different sizes too, indicating a mother and her cubs. And everyone knows the most dangerous of bears are a mother with cubs! But by the look on Dr. Trent's face, the bear would have been no match for her! The bright red hair didn't compare to the angry red face. She was livid! She holstered her pistol, kicked a table, and stomped back through the cave. Deuce could hear her on the walkie talkie, "Y'all come on down, everyone except Jemma. Have her go back to camp and get the rest of the rolls of string and any stakes we have left. Damn bears have trashed the grid!"

Deuce began folding up the tables and placing them to the side, trying to stay busy and out of Carrie's way. It was the first time he had seen her pissed off, and it wasn't a very pretty sight! Ronnie and Ben entered the cave and were relieved to see that most of their sections were still intact. The rest of the crew began straightening out the stakes and rolling up the tangled string. About the time Jemma showed up with the new string and stakes, Ben walked over to Dr. Trent and Yellow Wing.

"Hey Carrie, Yellow Wing, I have an idea on how to stop this from happening again."

"What's that Ben?" Carrie asked.

"Hows about Ronnie and I set up our tent out in front of the cave entrance. We could park a 4 wheeler in the mouth of the cave, and keep a fire going most of the night. That should keep the wildlife away," he answered. But what he was really thinking about was the privacy and extra time he and Ronnie would have for looking for the deeds with no one around.

"I was just thinking along those lines myself, Ben," said Dr. Trent, "but was wondering who to ask, so thanks for volunteering."

"No problem," he answered, and went to work setting up the tables and hammering stakes.

Most of the morning was spent repairing the damage, and by lunchtime they were actually digging and scanning with metal detectors. Deuce and Jemma were in section B, with 24 grids starting from the granite cliff face and extending ten yards west to the Bayonet Tree, ten yards north of the tree, and ten yards south of it. Deuce wanted to run the metal detector and dig wherever it went off. Jemma had to explain to him the reasons why they didn't work that way.

"We start against the rock face, grid one, and dig down 16-24 inches. This is the average amount of soil and detritus build up occurring over the period of time involved here. We go backwards, always keeping our holes in front of us. That way, we don't disturb them as we go and we keep them in order for easy cataloging. Oh, and you don't step in one and break your damn ankle a hundred miles from the nearest hospital!" As she said this, she laughed and held up her ankle, showing a long scar of stitches.

"One titanium rod and eight screws, 5 years ago, Gobi Desert!"

"Okay, you lead the way and I'll just dig where and when you tell me,"

Deuce said. Seemed to him they were taking all of the fun out of it, but it made sense and they were the pros.

By five o'clock that afternoon, Deuce was sore, cramped, and tired. He and Jemma had worked there way through grids 1-6 to a depth of 24 inches and had nothing to show for it but some lead shot and a brass button. Jemma re-assured him that tomorrow they would take the metal detector and start scanning everywhere they had dug. But for now, a cold beer and a country shower were all that was on her mind!

CHAPTER 16

THE BEAR FACTS

DEUCE SAT ASTRIDE his horse, enjoying the cool breeze and watching the first hint of sunrise force it's way through the trees and over the mountains. The early morning fog that gave these mountains the look for which they were named, was just starting to dissipate. He nudged the mare gently in the ribs with his foot and began the slow descent back down to the dig site. He was skirting the perimeter of the canyon from above, and was thinking that he needed to go for a ride every morning. It seemed like such a pleasant way to start the day. And, he thought would even be that much more pleasant if he had Yellow Wing for company.

He maneuvered the paint quietly through the brush, letting her set her own pace. Deuce was busy watching the ground for bear tracks, trying to determine from which way they had come to the canyon. If they had a den close by, there should be some sign or tracks leading back to it. He had thought it unusual that there were so many tracks inside the cave and canyon, yet so few outside of the cave entrance.

And no bear poop. Anywhere. He recalled his grandfather telling him once that bear were like a bull in a china shop. What they didn't break, they shit on! So there should be poop somewhere!

As he followed the few remaining tracks, they led into some brush, where he spotted some disturbed earth. He assumed that the bears had been digging for grubs, but as he looked closer, there were no claw marks, and once again, no poop! Only a single line of tracks led into the bushes, and no exiting tracks. Were the bears still in there? He dismounted cautiously and examined the area, discovering distinct brush marks over what he was sure were boot prints leading out of the bushes. What the hell? He crawled into the brush and began to examine the disturbed earth, expecting to find claw marks where the bear had been digging, only to find definite spade marks that clearly showed someone had buried something here. But he couldn't imagine what. He went back to his horse and got the camp shovel he always carried, went back and began to dig. He just knew he was going to feel like an idiot when he dug up a bag of excrement or feces that someone had buried. And when he discovered a black plastic trash bag, he nearly stopped digging, except there was something brown and furry visible through a tear in the bag. He continued digging until he could lift the bag out, and when he looked inside, he wasn't prepared for what he had found! Feet! And claws! Not just any feet and claws, but definitely black bear feet and claws! Also several bottles of bear urine. The kind bear hunters could order from any hunting magazine.

Then he heard voices. The digging teams were showing up and talking with Ben and Ronnie, making Deuce realize how close he was to their tent. He quickly reburied the bag and brushed his footprints away as he carefully backed out of the brush. He was already beginning to piece the puzzle together as to how the site at he canyon got destroyed, but for the life of him, he couldn't figure out why! He decided to keep this information to himself for the time being, at least until he could figure out the why part!

Deuce tied the mare to a tree and gave her some water in a bucket, then entered the cave. Ben and Ronnie were hard at work by the granite wall, digging up what would later be determined as more lead shot and bullet casings. Jemma looked up as he approached.

"Hey Deuce, get over here bro! Come check it out and see what I discovered already! Where ya been, anyway?"

Deuce walked over, put on his gloves and joined Jemma in the hole. He was surprised to see little yellow flags everywhere, indicating all of the hits she had gotten from the metal detector.

"I was just riding around and lost track of time. Man, is it ever beautiful back behind this canyon!"

"Yeah, cool, but come see what I have discovered back against the granite cliff."

She had gotten a strong hit right under the granite shelf, and as she was digging to find out what was there, had unearthed some skeletal remains. She had discovered a silver bracelet, still encircling some arm bones that she said were the ulna and radius. With careful digging, it took them roughly 2 hours to reveal the complete right side of a skeletal body, making it obvious that the body had been shoved under the granite shelf, then packed with rocks and covered with dirt, sealing it in. You could still see the holster and boot outlines, but when disturbed, they just turned to dust. The boot buckles and belt buckle were removed from the remains as well as the silver bracelet, and a gold chain and cross from the chest area. The pistol was missing, but the 36 caliber bullets lay among the bones of the pelvic region, obviously from the now disintegrated holster and belt. Jemma went to go find a carry board, a hard flat plastic board similar to what they transport patients on that have back or neck injuries. She explained how they would dig beneath the skeleton, and little by little, try to insert the board under it in hopes of removing the remains as much intact as possible. Deuce was once again impressed with her level of expertise.

"Who do you think it is?" asked Jemma.

Deuce looked the remains over, trying to remember a certain passage from Sargeant Comb's journal about where and how he buried Desmond after the young man had gave his life trying to defend him.

"I'm thinking it is probably Daniel Desmond. You remember, the one who had heard the other two talking about killing the sergeant?"

"Nope, don't recall that part," said Jemma. "You forget, I wasn't here when y'all started this."

"Oh, yeah. Well, you ought to read the Sergeant's journal. Pretty wild stuff. But, yeah, I'm almost certain it is Desmond's remains. Hopefully we can return them to some family members, as well as explain his disappearance and act of courage in defending the Sergeant. The other two, whom the Sergeant killed, he wrote they were drug away by horse to some field. I doubt we'll ever find anything of them."

All the while Deuce was talking, Jemma had continued digging and was now ready to try and slide the board under the remains. After only two attempts, they were successful in removing the skeleton mostly intact.

Once they had him on the table, everyone else shut down and came to view their first major find. Dr. Trent and Yellow Wing began the task of trying to re-assemble what bones had come loose and mixed with all of the dirt and debris. The grids they had been working on had yet to yield anything other than a few brass buttons. Deuce and Jemma returned to their sections and used the metal detector some more, but only came up with a few more items that were unidentifiable at the moment. The rest of the day was spent examining the remains of Daniel Desmond.

CHAPTER 17

A Puzzle for Ronnie and Ben

RONNIE AND BEN had finished their search of the cave floor and discovered little of interest, other than a small pocketknife and a tin cup. At least that's what they told everyone else. After exiting the cave, they were now working grid G, sections 4 and 8, which were immediately outside of the inner cave exit and against the granite wall. Even though they had discovered little of historical value inside the cave, they had found more etchings carved into the cave wall, all by the exit leading into the canyon. Ben was convinced that they were clues leading either to the gold or the maps. Ronnie wasn't quite so sure, but either way, he had agreed not to mention it to anyone else.

As the rest of the team left for their base camp, Ben began to do a systematic search with the metal detector, concentrating on the granite wall area adjacent to the cave opening. The markings they had found had taken them about an hour to decipher, and Ronnie was still thinking it was a WAG. (Acronym for wild ass guess). The new markings were discovered only a few feet away from the cave exit, and not more than 10 feet from where Deuce had unearthed the brass cylinder with the Sergeant's journal in it. The markings Deuce had discovered were all 2 or 3 feet above the floor of the cave, indicating they may have been etched from a sitting position. The ones that Ben had found were only inches from the floor, and most likely done from a flat or prone position. The Sergeant may not have had the strength left to raise his arms very high, or may have intentionally placed them that low.

The first etching was of another box with an arrow attached pointing to the cave exit, or south. In the center of the box, Ben was convinced that the letter G was inscribed. Ronnie wasn't quite so sure, thinking it looked more like a 5, or maybe a 6. The second mark also resembled a box with an arrow attached, only this time, the arrow pointed up and definitely had the number 10 inscribed within. But after nearly a century and a half of erosion, even protected from the environment by the cave, it was still difficult to tell what the third box indicated.

After several cleanings and dusting with powder, it still remained incomprehensible to them both. It too, was a box with an arrow in it, pointing down this time. There were no numbers that were legible in this one, only a bunch of what looked like small half circles and 2 curved lines. One curving left, and one curving right, and both coming from the center of the half circles and protruding an inch below them. To Ronnie, it had first seemed like a cat track, or maybe a bear paw, but that made no sense. As he stared at the paper they had drawn the etchings on, Ronnie began a slow laugh that increased to a full blown chuckle.

"Look here, Ben! We are going about this the wrong way, from the wrong direction! The first box Deuce discovered pointed us to these. The box with an arrow pointing towards the cave exit, and a round circle in the middle with a 20 in the circle, right? 20 dollar gold piece? So, could the first box we discovered actually be a 6 instead of a G for gold? Indicating we go 6 paces in the direction south; instead of the next arrow pointing up, what if it meant we go right, or east 10 paces?"

"And the third box?" asked Ben.

Ronnie could no longer contain himself, "It's a tree! A kid's drawing of a damn tree! With an arrow pointing to the bottom of the frigging tree!"

Ben studied the drawings for a few minutes, then started laughing along with Ronnie. "By God, you just might have something! Let's get the metal detector and start stepping this puppy off!"

Ronnie stood in the mouth of the cave, prepared to take 6 steps, when Ben reminded him that the Sargeant had been severely wounded in the hip, so his steps may not have been as far as normal. Ronnie shortened his stride a bit and counted off 6 paces, then planted a red flag. Turning to his right, he stepped off 10 paces, which brought him right to the base of the granite cliff. But no tree. In fact there were no trees in either direction until the Bayonet tree 30 feet away. Ronnie placed another flag at the base of the cliff face and walked back to where Ben stood with a puzzled look on his face.

"Man, I was so sure you were right! I would have bet on it!" But Ben had no sooner said that, when Ronnie punched him on the arm and said, "Look up, man! Up!" Ben looked up and realized what Ronnie was looking at. What had probably been a small oak sapling growing out of a crack a 140 something years ago, was now a huge arboreal canopy that was partially responsible for the canyon's seclusion.

Ben put his headphones on, turned on the metal detector and began to sweep from left to right in front of the granite face. As he did this, Ronnie began to figure out that there was probably a cavity similar to the one where Desmond's remains had been found. In fact, the cavity most likely ran the full length of the granite wall. Just as he was about to share this information with Ben, the detector began to make the high pitched squeal that was reserved for precious metals! Ben dropped to his knees and began to carefully dig in front of the cliff.

"Try digging down and then under the cliff face," Ronnie suggested. Ben began to prod the ground at the base of the cliff, and sure enough, there was another cavity. He took the pin-pointer wand attached to the detector and waved it in front of the cavity. The squeal got louder and more high pitched. Ronnie joined him with his mini spade and within ten minutes they had excavated a 2 foot by 4 foot wide area.

"Look! Look right here! What is that, man? See it…right there!" As Ronnie looked closer, he could see what could only be deteriorated wood fragments. He began to use his hands and in minutes had dislodged all of the rotted wood. He took a small paintbrush and swept the dirt away. He grabbed a water bottle and poured some into the hole, brushing once more, and began laughing as the bright yellow color of stacked gold coins began to shine through the dirt. Ben was about to dive in with his shovel, all his training in archaeology forgotten as the gold fever took him.

"Wait, wait, man! Hold on a sec, bro! We need to take it slow and easy and try to recover everything before we move it! You know the drill, man!"

"Yeah, I know, Ronnie. But what if the maps and deeds are buried here too? We have to get to them before the others do!"

"Yeah, yeah, I know, but all the more reason to do it right. It would look awfully suspicious if we didn't abide by our training, wouldn't it? Besides, we have all night, man."

They began to slowly unearth the gold coins and when they had uncovered them all, they found that there were 5 pieces per stack, and 16 stacks of nothing but 20 dollar Lady Liberty gold coins. Ronnie had brought a large cardboard box back when he had gone after the lanterns. They sat the coins down in the box in the exact order that they removed them. Another 20 minutes of searching turned up nothing more than the rusted remain of an old lock and what might have once been the handles of the box. Ronnie was thinking about the gold coins. He knew a little about them from a cousin who was a numismatic enthusiast. Ronnie had asked, "What in the hell is that?" He had smiled and said "someone who likes old coins." So he knew a little bit about the Lady Liberty coins from 1850 to 1904. They were worth about 1300 hundred each, easily, but the historical value of these should supercede the numismatic value. And besides, they should belong to the descendants of the Cherokee braves who had earned them!

"So Ronnie, how are we going to do this? Should we try and cover up the hole, stay quiet about our find for now, or go ahead and tell everyone in the morning?"

Ronnie stared at Ben for a moment before he answered. Surely the guy wasn't that stupid? Anyone with any sense would be able to tell that some digging had been going on, even if they did try to cover it up. And while he had agreed to help destroy or steal the land deeds if found, that was as far as he was willing to go.

"I say we turn them in tomorrow and show everybody what we found. But first, let's take a real close look at the coins. Something isn't adding up here. All the clues in the cave led us to the gold, but why are there no clues to where the maps are hidden? It's like he wanted us to find the coins first. Surely he didn't just put a note or map in the box, knowing it would deteriorate over time."

Ben reached in the box and picked up a coin from the top of the first stack. Taking a clean brush and some soap and water, he cleaned and polished it to a bright lustrous yellow. He took the magnifying glass and studied the coin, starting with the Lady Liberty side first. There was nothing apparent, so he turned it over and discovered the back was so ornately inscribed that there was no room for any king of markings. He and Ronnie repeated the process through the 4 of the 16 stacks, finding nothing out of the ordinary.

"What if we started from the wrong end?" Ronnie asked, as he picked up the top coin from the other corner of the box. He repeated their cleaning process and was immediately rewarded by finding a square box with an arrow attached. "Here we go again with the damn arrows and boxes!" he shouted.

Ronnie figured that this time, if you held the Lady Liberty profile so it was looking straight to your left, and you faced the granite wall, the arrow was pointing due south. He was sure that the inscription inside the box was definitely a G, maybe standing for where they had found the gold. The second coin had a box with a south pointing arrow and the number 10 in it. Okay, thought Ronnie, 10 steps south along the granite wall. With Ben looking over his shoulder, he cleaned the third coin and discovered a box with an arrow pointing east and the letter M and number 7 beside it. He shrugged his shoulders.

"What, maybe map number 7, or 7 maps or cases?"

"Could be, though we don't know how many map cases there should be," answered Ben. Ronnie picked up the fourth coin. After cleaning it, he was looking at a box and arrow pointing south again, and beneath that, the number 5.

"Keep going," Ben said, "then we'll lay them all out in order and try to figure them out." Ronnie picked up the fifth and last coin in that stack. It too, had a box and an arrow, pointing east again, and the letter M and the number 10 in it. With all 5 laid out in order, he started on the next stack. An hour later, he and Ben had finished cleaning the remaining 54 coins. There were no more marks found on any coins, so now they concentrated on deciphering Sergeant Comb's clues.

Ronnie stared at the coins and said, "All right, let's start with the first one and use what we know so far. Let's assume the G stands for gold and the Lady has to be facing south. The second coin could mean south 10 steps. The third coin points east again, possibly meaning against or under the granite face, like the gold was. The M may stand for maps or map cases, the number 7 for how many are there."

"Don't forget," Ben said, "The Sarge was in really bad shape, so he was looking for the easiest place to hide them. There may have been several openings under that granite face, and all he had to do was fill them in with rocks and dirt, then let Mother Nature do the rest."

"Right, so if there are 7 buried there, then the fourth coin means …what?"

Ben studied the fourth coin. The box had an arrow pointing south again, the M and 7 again, but with a 5 under it.

"Okay, I think I've got it! Just like the coin with the G, let's assume the 5 stands for steps south from the M7 location. Then the last coin would once more mean against or under the granite face, and the M 10 means 10 more maps or cases!"

"Well, buddy, what the hell are we waiting on?" asked Ronnie. "Lets get the damn metal detector and get to work!"

CHAPTER 18

THE COST OF KNOWING THINGS

DEUCE HAD NOW gotten into the habit of taking the old paint mare out for a ride after supper each evening. The beauty and majesty of the surrounding hills and valleys, were only magnified by the setting sun. It also gave him time to reflect on the past and imagine the future. A way to relax after a day of manual labor, or at least that's what he told Yellow Wing and Dr. Trent. After his discovery the day before yesterday of the bear claws and paws, as well as the tracks leading away from the area, he knew something strange was going on, but he just couldn't imagine what. Was there someone trying to scare them off, and if so, who and why? He had seen the anger and frustration from Dr. Trent when the site had been wrecked, so if she had anything to do with it, she deserved an Oscar for her performance! And there was no way that he could bring himself to think Yellow Wing had anything to do with it. But how well did he really know her?

While he pondered these questions, he more or less let the horse have free rein, and after a bit, the old horse had taken him up a trail that came out above the canyon. It was still awhile until sunset proper, but he figured they had better start back. Riding in the dark on a moonlit trail didn't bother him or the paint, but up here along the canyon's rim, it was just testing fate. As he headed back down the trail to the clearing, he heard an excited yell, then loud laughter and a very animated conversation. He couldn't make out exactly what they were saying, but the canyon created an echo that was easily heard, especially if you were above it.

Deuce recognized Ronnie's voice, and it was clear that they had found something interesting. It was still light enough, and he figured he had about another hour of daylight left. Enough time that he could drop in on the guys and see what all of the excitement was about. He also decided to walk the mare the last few hundred yards, maybe take a look around before making his presence known. Deuce found it hard to believe that Ronnie could be involved in anything shady, but there was something about Ben that just didn't sit right with him. If anyone here had anything to do with the fake bear tracks, Deuce was willing to bet it would be Ben.

"6, 7, 8, 9, 10! Okay, let's try it right here," Ronnie said to Ben.

Ben hurried over with the metal detector and began to sweep 5 feet to either side of Ronnie's mark. As he got closer to the granite wall, he began to hear a faint change in the tone of the machine. When he was right against the wall, the tone loudened and became a steady squeal! Ronnie dropped to his knees and began to dig down a foot, then dug a foot towards the wall. Sure enough, there was another opening beneath the ledge, filled in with small rocks and dirt. After only 5 minutes of digging and removing rocks, Ronnie struck something hard and could see a yellow scratch on what he had hit! In a few more minutes with a small spade and brush, he discovered a cylindrical object staring him, the brass shining through the dirt where he had hit it with the spade.

Ronnie let out a wild yell and began laughing. Ben was jumping up and down and laughing with him! For a few minutes, the thrill of the discovery had made Ronnie forget the betrayal he had agreed to. They spent the next hour slowly excavating the area, and discovered 7 brass containers, all still perfectly sealed.

"Well, now what, Ben? Do we open them and see what's inside, or do we find the others first?"

"Hmmm, let's find the others first. If we open only a few before we find the deeds, they won't be nearly as mad as they would if we opened them all! If we have all of the containers, there may be a way to tell which one has the deeds in it. Maybe it's marked or smaller than the others, something different?"

Ronnie thought for a minute. "Right, right. So we have to go 5 steps further down? 1, 2, 3, 4, 5. About here!"

Once again, Ben began to work the metal detector, and in about 10 minutes, he and Ronnie were shouting again as they carefully removed the remaining 10 map containers! "Okay, Ronnie, let's carry all of these over to the tent where we can check them out thoroughly, see if they are numbered or marked in any way. I doubt they are, or if they were, the marks would have been on the leather, which has rotted away years ago. But who knows? Let's go see!"

They moved to a table in the tent and laid out all 17map cases. Ben took a wet rag and started cleaning the dirt off, while Ronnie examined each one closely, looking for any kind of mark that would indicate which one held the deeds. After they had examined each one, they hadn't found anything to convince them as to which one to open first. Ben was already trying to come up with a reasonable explanation for having opened them all. It was going to be hard to explain to Dr. Trent and Yellow Wing.

Ronnie had one last idea. With all of them lying side by side, he noticed that there were 2 of them that were shorter than the rest. As he compared their weight by holding one in each hand, he concluded that one of the shorter ones was lighter than the rest. He remembered hearing somewhere that most of the maps were probably done on animal hides, so naturally they would be heavier than parchment paper.

"So, what do you think? Should we try this one first?" asked Ronnie.

"Yeah, go for it man!" answered Ben, with a maniacal grin on his face. Ronnie then took a hammer and chisel and forced the end off!

Deuce had tied the horse to a tree a couple of hundred feet from the cave entrance. As he followed the trail down, he could hear the guys yelling and laughing in their tent. He decided to ease into the thicket behind their tent and listen for a minute to see if he could determine what all of the excitement was about, before making his presence known. All he heard Ronnie say was something about a bonus and them being the luckiest bastards in the world to have found them. Them who, he wondered? The maps? Did they find them? Then he heard Ben say something about opening one. Knowing how upset Dr. Trent and Yellow Wing would be for them not following protocol, he was about to walk up and tell them not to open it. Then he heard something behind him. He turned just quick enough to see the shovel coming down on him!

Deuce opened his left eye and slowly looked around. The bass drum pounding in his head was keeping perfect rhythm with his heart, and the flashing lights were perfectly choreographed in sync with the drum. He tried to open his right eye, only to discover it was full of sand, and when he tried to raise his right hand to brush the sand out, it wouldn't move. Neither would his left. He began to hear noises that were getting elevated and becoming more like voices in a heated conversation. Then, through the cacophony of drums and flashing lights, the pain made itself properly known. He closed his eye again, wincing in pain, and his memory started to slowly return. He figured his best course of action was to remain still and listen to what was being said.

CHAPTER 19

From a Thief to a Murderer

"**W**HAT THE HELL did you do, Ben! Are you out of your damn mind!?"

"Just what was I supposed to do, man? He was squatting there, right behind the damn tent! Son of a bitch heard everything we said! He knows it all! We have got to get rid of him somehow! And the horse, what about his freaking horse? Man, we have to take him somewhere, maybe push him and his horse off a tall cliff! But we gotta do something quick!"

"Hold on a minute, Ben! I agreed to help you find the damn deeds and make them disappear. That's done! I'm done! I didn't sign up for murder! Give me my other 5 grand and I'm outta here!"

"And go where, Ronnie? 10 grand won't get you far, especially when the cops are looking for you! And we're on Federal land, so you're talking F.B.I.! Where are you going to go where they can't find you? First place they are going to look, is on any reservation where you have friends or relatives! Then everyone will know that you cheated your own people, and who's going to take your side over Deuce and Yellow Wing? And what about me? My whole life is in the Knoxville area! We don't have a choice, man!"

"Oh, dammit, Ben! Damn, damn, damn! Okay, okay, let me think! We gotta plan this right! We just CANNOT get caught! It has to look like an accident, even better if he is never found at all! Oh man oh man, I can't believe this shit you got me into!"

Ronnie collapsed on the ground, crossed his legs and hung his head in his hands. Ben just stood there, hands on hips, staring blankly at the brass tubes and dirt on the table. Their guesswork had paid off, and the first cylinder they opened, the smallest and lightest one, had contained the documents and deeds from the Department of Land Management. All they required was the signatures from the tribal elders and the land south and east of the reservation would have been theirs. All of it was once in Confederate states, so with the Union winning the war, they would have cared less who they had to displace to make it tribal land again. Sergeant Combs and his men had forever altered the course of history for the Cherokee, and stopped the reshaping of the borders of Alabama, Tennessee, and North Carolina. And hardly anyone had ever known what had been done! Though Ronnie and Ben hadn't had time to examine the paperwork properly, a quick perusal had shown them that Trowbridge Forest Products, Inc. had plenty to worry about if the deeds were taken to court or contested!

Deuce remained perfectly still as he listened to them debate his fate. He couldn't believe what he was hearing! That Ronnie had been prepared to cheat his own people was shocking enough, but was now considering murder, too? Deuce's only hope lie with his ability to free himself, and that all depended on how seriously he was hurt. Having been afraid to move, he couldn't determine his strength level and could only hope that when the opportunity presented itself, he would know what to do and have the energy to do it! He knew he was no action hero, had no self defense training, no military training, and his only advantage was his size. He was quite a bit bigger than either of them, and his only other hope was surprise and to get his hands on some kind of weapon.

When Ronnie and Ben left the tent to go find his horse, Deuce began testing the knots and the rope that was binding his hands together. He was hoping that Ben had tied the knots, as Ronnie was probably more familiar with different types of securement from working with horses and re-creating tepees and other Indian artifacts. Just as he thought the ropes were finally loosening, Ben entered the tent carrying the trash bag full of bear paws and claws. As soon as Deuce seen them, his imagination sent shivers of fear down his spine! What kind of sick plan had Ben come up with?

The razor sharp claws and the bear urine had given Ben an idea, if he could only talk Ronnie into it. When he returned with the horse, Ben began to explain his idea.

"First off, we need to erase the boot prints he left from where he hid his horse, and then up to the tent. And the drag marks from me hauling him in here. Then the hoof prints of the horse, and we need to hurry. When he doesn't return tonight, they're going to start looking for him, and eventually come here! If not tonight, then in the morning, for sure. So, my first question for you, is do you know of a place where we can hide him for at least a day?"

Ronnie stared at the bear claws, then at Ben, then looked at Deuce before he answered. "Yeah, maybe. 4 or 5 miles from here. Take about 2 hours to walk there, then longer coming back because I'll have to erase our tracks."

"So, it's 8:30. We can be there by midnight, and back here before daylight?" asked Ben. "Most likely. But what kind of bull are thinking to pull off with those claws and paws?" questioned Ronnie.

"Listen Ronnie. I know you don't want to do this. Hell, man, neither do I! But we have to do it! He might be severely concussed already from the shovel to the head. He hasn't moved since I hit him! We take him to where you know there are bears often. I'll take these claws and cut him up some. Probably have to gag him and hit him again. But we kill the horse by cutting its throat, then use the bear claws to cover up the cut. We can make the horse actually fall on him and pin him down, then hope the blood draws the bears in the area. A little bit of this female bear urine should help, too. With any luck, the bears will get rid of any evidence of us hitting him or killing the horse! So, what do you think?"

"Ben, you are an evil bastard. That's what I think!" answered Ronnie.

"Okay genius, you got any better ideas? Besides, we need to take the map case with the deeds and hide them. Then I'll call Mr. Trowbridge and let him know we found them, and tell him we're going to need that bonus pretty quick!"

"Well, hell Ben. I ain't got any better ideas to contribute, so if we're going to do this, then let's get to it before I change my mind!"

As Deuce lay listening to Ben's plan, a cold chill began to run down his spine again as his mind raced 90 to nothing. How was he going to over power both of them? Should he continue to act unconscious so they wouldn't hurt him again, or should he speak up, try to talk them out of it? He just knew Ronnie and Ben would most likely get caught, but a lot of good that would do him if he was already dead! He had always considered himself to be an above average intelligence, and somewhat macho type, but now that his life depended on his intelligence and brawn, he didn't feel all that smart or tough! The wrong move and failure could mean death! He decided to remain immobile and let them try to initiate their plan, hoping that an opportinity would present itself. Hoping that when he didn't return to camp, that they would start looking for him. Surely someone had noticed his absence by now?

Yellow Wing was tired. Tired of everyone else finding things. Tired of Carrie's smarter than you attitude. Tired of thinking about Deuce and his tight blue jeans. Tired of stopping herself from falling for him. She wanted to sneak into his tent, crawl into his sleeping bag, and do things that made her blush just thinking about it! But she didn't want to do that just once. No, she wanted to do that every night for the rest of her life! With all of these thoughts running through her mind, even running through her body, she was afraid to see him tonight. She didn't know if she could contain her emotions. She just knew that she would say the wrong thing, do the wrong thing, or that he would take advantage of her emotions, then reject her later. And, as with most strong willed, intelligent women, she couldn't stand the thought of being used. Or rejected. So, she just remained in her tent with her thoughts of love and sex, and never noticed that Deuce hadn't returned from his evening ride....

+ ◆ ◆ ◆ ◆ +

Ronnie and Ben stood looking down at Deuce.

"Damn Ben, you may have already killed him! He hasn't moved since you brought him in!"

"Check his pulse, Ron, you know, under his chin, on his throat, like on CSI. I'll stand back with the shovel in case he moves. Wait! Doesn't he always have a pistol with him in his saddlebags? Go get it! I'll watch him while you go. We need to load him on the horse anyway!"

"Right, right, okay, I'll be back in a few."

Deuce lie there thinking that maybe this was his chance, with Ronnie gone. If Ben would just get closer, maybe reach down to see if he was still alive, too impatient to wait on Ronnie. He thought he might have the ropes loose enough to get his hands free. But no, Ben kept his distance. He walked over to the table and was looking at the map cases. Maybe he would keep his back turned, thought Deuce. I'll jump up and body slam him, I'll…Oh shit, thought Deuce! Ben had turned around and raised the shovel and was about to hit him again!

"Ben!" yelled Ronnie. "What the hell, man! Put down that damn shovel! There isn't a bear alive that would leave that kind of injury on his skull! Are you trying to get us caught?"

"Okay, man, okay, I just thought I saw him staring at me! I just wanted to make sure he was out!"

"Dumb ass! If you kill him now, he won't bleed right when the bears get to him! Forensics would be able to tell he was already dead before the bear attack!"

"Yeah, right, right. Did you find the gun?"

"I found it. Now I'm going to hold the gun on him while you go and see if he is still alive. God, I hope so!

Ben leaned down beside Deuce and stuck his fingers up against his throat and carotid artery, feeling for the steady throb. Deuce wanted to slow his rapid heart rate down, but to no avail.

"It's beating really fast! Is that good?" asked Ben.

"Yeah, I guess. At least we know he is still alive. Let's tie him up better and load him onto the horse. It'll take us about an hour or so to get there. Maybe longer, now that it's gotten dark. You have to come with me, man. It's your plan, your idea, so you get to kill the horse!"

Deuce had seen movies where people had been thrown sideways over a saddle. He had never realized the agony they went through. Why ever think about something like that? He had never realized how uncomfortable it might be. After about a mile, his stomach and kidneys felt as if he were laying on barbed wire. He was doing his best not to moan, not to scream as the pain worsened. He just prayed that wherever they were going, they would get there soon! But so far, he was still alive, and the pain and circumstances were really starting to piss him off! All he could think about through the pain; was if I ever get my hands on these assholes! He knew he wasn't a natural born killer, and had never even entertained the thought of killing someone. But his thoughts were changing.

CHAPTER 20

BEAR BAIT

"R ED?"

"Yeah, who is this?"

"It's me cousin, Yellow Wing! I need your help! Deuce has disappeared!"

"What? You're going to have to speak up! I'm in the plane, and you sound like you're in a barrel! Who hit a deer?"

"I'm on a satphone, Red. And it's Deuce! He is missing and I need your help to look for him!"

"Deuce is missing? From where? I thought you guys were playing in the dirt down by Plott's Basin? You 2 get in a lover's spat and he take off on you?"

"No, Red, nothing like that! He went for a ride yesterday evening and has never come back! He wasn't in his tent this morning and his horse isn't here either! We have been looking for him all morning, and Ronnie found some tracks on the south side of Angel's Rest, along a high ridge and they just end suddenly! Red, I'm really getting worried!"

"Okay, okay, cuz, just calm down! I'm sure he's all right. I'm just now flying in from Charlotte. I'll circle back and do a few flyovers, see if I can spot anything, then I'll hop in a truck and head your way with some more horses and help. Just stay cool and search in pairs. We don't need anyone else getting lost or hurt trying to find him!"

"All right, Red. But hurry, please!"

"Sure cuz, and if he hasn't turned up by the time I get there, I'll call out half of the Cherokee Nation to look for him!"

Ronnie was so tired he could barely sit up in the saddle. He had closed his eyes for just a few minutes, maybe an hour at the most, when Yellow Wing had showed up looking for Deuce. It had taken them a lot longer to move through the woods at night than he had expected. He then had to erase their tracks on the return, and he wasn't sure how good of a job he had done, so he had went back at first light. He was able to erase a few more tracks he had missed earlier, but he still wasn't satisfied that he had gotten them all. So when Yellow Wing called on him to help search, he had quickly volunteered to take the other horse and search to the north, the direction from which they had come after dumping Deuce and his horse. That would at least explain why there were horse tracks going in that direction, and give him time to cover up anything he had missed earlier.

Now he was south of the river and marking off areas on the search grid as having already been thoroughly searched. He had found some old tracks and followed them onto a rock strewn ledge where the tracks stopped and turned around. He had managed to obscure the other tracks with his own horse, enough so that no one would be able to tell where Deuce had turned around. His hopes were that they would think Deuce's horse had slipped off of the edge of the canyon rim and fallen into the chasm below.

While Ronnie and most of the crew were searching for Deuce, Ben had shown Dr. Trent the gold and the map cases they had discovered, and she was ecstatic! All concerns for a missing lawyer went by the wayside, and the maps took precedence! Besides, she figured Deuce would come strolling in with a lame horse or some such other excuse, and they had dozens more of his cousins with horses coming to look for him, so they sure didn't need her! Carrie figured her responsibility was to get the map cases and gold coins to the University and into the Professor's hands. Ben and Ronnie had done a remarkable job of finding the coins, then deciphering the clues to where the map cases were buried. She could hardly believe that he and Ronnie had done all of that work in less then 36 hours! She asked him why they didn't stop and come get her and the rest of the team? Ben had explained that once the clues started coming together, they forgot everything else and just couldn't stop searching! And Carrie knew how the adrenaline and excitement could overwhelm you, even sustain you for hours of labor. But also, she had been all over the world and had worked with people of all colors, all cultures, and all vices! She could tell that there had been something other than adrenalin fueling his endeavors. He was exhibiting all the classic signs of a cocaine or amphetamine hangover; the red eyes, nervous twitches, slurred speech, etc. It was for that reason she had agreed to take him with her when he asked to come along with her to Knoxville. He looked like he needed a break!

When they arrived at the university, Professor Hartshorne met them in the parking lot with 3 grocery carts to haul all of the map cases and box of gold coins. As they loaded them in the carts, Professor Hartshorne inquired as to why Deuce and Yellow Wing had not joined them? Carrie then began to explain about Deuce being missing, after which he had replied,

"Well, my dear, I am just as anxious as you are to have a look at these mythical maps, but I think that out of professional courtesy, we should wait on their arrival before opening any of them. Instead, let's concentrate on the coins and pictures of the wall etchings that Mr. Hackett here has deciphered. Ben, you do know that I'm going to require a detailed report describing you and Ronnie's procedures and intuitions that led you to the discovery of the gold, and then how you processed that information and found the map cases!"

Ben was standing off to one side, not paying much attention to the conversation. His mind was still reeling from the strenuous night and no sleep, and worse still, no more coke! He just wanted to get home, get rid of these bloodstained clothes in his backpack, and try to get some sleep. Try to get the images out of his head of all of that blood, and try to get the awful screaming sound of the dying horse out of his mind!

When he looked up, he found the Professor and Dr. Trent staring at him as he nervously fidgeted in place, and realized that they had been talking to him.

"Yes sir," he stammered, not quite sure what ha been said. "I think I'd better get home and get some rest, sir. It's been a long strenuous week, and I'm exhausted." With that said, he abruptly turned and walked to his car.

When Deuce came to, the first thing that he noticed was the smell, then the pain. His ears were ringing and his vision was blurry, but it seemed his olfactory senses were working overtime. The horses blood and urine were all over him, as well as his own. What bit of moonlight showing through the canopy did little to help his blurry vision determine how dire his situation really was. As he lay there taking deep breaths and fighting off the nausea, the previous nights events began to unfold in his pain ravaged mind. He remembered being draped over his horse's saddle, and the intense pain of the trek through the woods. When the horse had finally stopped moving, his midsections were so sore, and his legs felt as if a thousand ants were biting him all at once. He knew there was no way he could stand, and if he couldn't stand, how was he going to stop them from killing him? He was hoping they would take him off of the horse, maybe debate what they were going to do next, give him a chance to catch his breath, then come up with some idea as to what he was going to do.

As he was trying to think this through, Ben had untied the rope that bound his feet and hands together beneath the horse's belly, causing him to unceremoniously flop to the ground. Try as he might, he couldn't stop himself from letting out a loud groan of agony, followed by an 'Oh shit' as he hit the ground. The loud exclamation startled both Ronnie and Ben, causing the latter to once again grab his shovel and waylay Deuce across the back of the head! His last clear thought had been, not again! After that, he recalled very little, except for a horrendous screaming noise, then something hot and wet soaking his face and body! And more pain, enough pain to make him momentarily forget his pounding head. Such instantaneous pain in his lower extremities, legs, hips, and groin! And as he remembered that awful pain, of course it began to return! He continued to take slow steady breaths, as his legs and head now throbbed in concert. He now knew why he couldn't focus, as the tears of pain flowed from his eyes. When he finally got up the stamina and courage to try and move, the overwhelming pain caused him to blackout again. An act of the mind and its merciful wisdom!

As he came to the second time, or was it the third, it was like reading a familiar book over again. It only took a few pages for the whole story to return. The new position of the half-moon provided a little more light, allowing him to see just how precarious his situation really was. The only positive discovery he made was finding out that his hands and feet were no longer bound. But a lot of good they were going to do, for the moonlight had also revealed just what he had thought. There was 1500 pounds of dead horse lying on him from about his navel on down. When he tried to move his hips, excruciating pain once again engulfed him. He was now pretty sure that one or both legs were broken, and maybe a hip or pelvis bone, too! As he felt around, he found a multitude of large lacerations on the horse's torso, starting just in front of the saddle. As far as he could reach towards the horse's neck, there were gaping wounds soaked with the sticky coagulated blood now the consistency of syrup. Why, wondered Deuce, would anyone butcher a horse to such a degree? Were Ronnie and Ben so sick as to have done it for the thrill?

While he lie there trying to wrap his befuddled mind around such a barbaric act, he began to recall a conversation he had overheard between Ronnie and Ben. As if the broken legs and concussion weren't enough, now a cold shiver began to set into his spine. Ben's last sentence began to repeat itself like some old album stuck on a scratch..." Now we just let the hogs and bears finish our work for us...finish our work for us...finish our work for us...

CHAPTER 21

GRANDFATHER JOINS THE SEARCH

B Y 10 A.M., the search parties had covered most of a 2 mile wide by 4 mile long, area from the camp to the dig site, and mostly south of the canyon. That was where Deuce usually liked to ride. Ronnie had skirted the area north of the box canyon for a couple of miles, reporting no obvious tracks going that way. There were plenty of tracks in the southern area, but no one was talented enough to determine whether they were new or old tracks.

When Red showed up about noon, he was pulling a 4 horse trailer and had 2 of his buddies from the reservation's Search and Rescue Team with him. And sitting up front in the pick-up was none other than Grandfather. Red had tried to argue with the old man, saying how dangerous this back country was, and that they were quite confident they could find him, and he needn't come. Yeah, like that was going to happen! Grandfather then had to remind him who it was that had taught or trained most of the Search and Rescue Team on how to track animals and people! And also who had taught Deuce and Red!

"And yes, young man, I do know my eyesight is not what it used to be, but you people rely too much on just your eyesight. When tracking, you must use your ears and nose, too, both of which still happen to work just fine! I can no longer see those 2 flies fornicating in the top of that tree, but

I can hear them! And since you think I am so old and frail, go unload my horse and saddle it for me!"

Red and Grandfather were examining the aerial topography maps that the Search and Rescue Team had brought, when Ronnie came riding back into camp. Red waved him over, and when he approached, asked him to show then where he had already searched. They compared his map to theirs and circled in red the areas he claimed to have searched. Grandfather pulled a large magnifying glass from one of his many pockets and proceeded to examine the maps and co-ordinates closely. The look on his face dared anyone to comment on the visual aid.

While they poured over the maps, 4 more of the S & R Team arrived and informed Red that the helicopter would be on station within an hour or so. Only Ronnie knew how useless the chopper was going to be. Deuce's location would be nearly impossible to see from above due to the thick foliage and trees surrounding the spot where they had left him. Though he knew Deuce would be found eventually, his main goal had been to deter the searchers long enough for the bears and hogs to do their business. And he was exhausted, so he excused himself and told Red he was going get a few hours sleep. If they needed him, he would be in his tent down by the canyon. As he rode off on a 4 wheeler, Red turned to Grandfather and said,

"I don't like him, never have, and I'm not very confident in his tracking ability. What do you think about you and I re-visiting the areas he searched?"

Grandfather looked up at Red, one eye magnified to the size of a coffee cup.

"I taught all of you how to track," he said, as he pointed to the men around the table, "so I know you are good. I did not teach him, so I know he is not as good." To an outsider, it may have sounded like a boast, but to the men at the table, they knew it was just a fact.

"Red, let's you and I start from right here. All these extra people have done is to obscure the tracks. We know Deuce is not stupid. He wouldn't go too far, or into really rugged areas so close to sundown. So the only reason he hasn't shown up by now, is that he must be injured, and his horse, too. That old paint would have come straight back here if she could, with or without him. If something happened to the horse, and Deuce is hurt, he is going to find somewhere to hole up until we find him. And look for smoke. If he is able, he will light a fire and hope we see it."

"In the old days, very few off our horses were shod and their hoof prints were as individual as finger prints. But now days, they all have shoes. Little George is our farrier at the reservation. I'm sure you all know him. What you may not know, is that he always leaves a certain mark on at least one shoe. This trait goes back centuries, allowing the sheriffs of Europe to track horse thieves easier. The Army used to do it so they could track the tribes back to their villages, when ever they stole their horses. Little George always leaves one nail folded over on a certain shoe, as his mark. With 8 holes to a shoe, 4 shoes per horse, and 16 directions per shoe, and so on, he can put a different mark on hundreds of horses. I have already looked at the tracks where they keep the 2 horses at night. We need to look at Ronnie's horse and find Little George's mark and compare it to the paint. There will be a difference."

As he was saying this, he began to walk over to the rope pen where Ronnie had left the roan, still saddled in case someone else wanted to use it in the search. When Grandfather approached the roan, he turned to Red and said, "Have someone unsaddle her. We will not be using her any longer, once we determine the ferrier's mark. That will enable us to see where Ronnie has gone in his search and not confuse us in our tracking."

Grandfather knelt down and rasied up the roan's front left hoof, all the while quietly talking to the horse in Cherokee. He repeated the process on the left rear, then moved to the other side. When he examined the right rear hoof, he found there were 2 nails in one hole, one not all the way in and bent over flat, pointing rearwards. He then showed everyone.

"This is Little George's mark. Now that we know mark the roan has, we can look for the mark from the paint."

Due to all of the activity, it took a few minutes to find a clear set of tracks from the paint, and when they did, Grandfather showed them a track from the right front shoe. On the left side of the shoe, third hole from the bottom, was the 2 nail bent mark, pointing forward.

Grandfather made sure all of the trackers saw it, then told Red to take a picture with his phone and send it to all of the search teams phones to use as a reference in the field.

As more Search and Rescue Team members showed up, the areas were marked off and divided up to each duo of searchers. The civilians from the dig teams were asked to stay in camp and get their well-deserved rest. "Let the pros take over" was how Red had put it. Grandfather had told him "Get the idiots out of the way." The only concession was Yellow Wing. She refused to stay in camp! Red had known the argument was coming, and had wanted Grandfather to talk to her, convince her to stay. Amazingly, the old man was nowhere to be found! After Red had lost the argument with his cousin, they had borrowed a horse from the S&R Team. As she saddled the horse, with the help of 3 of the S&R team members, Grandfather magically appeared again.

"And just where were you when I needed you?" asked Red.

"Had to relieve myself. But you did good there for awhile, and even with my infinite wisdom, I fear the outcome would have been much the same! And I would rather have her mad at you than me. She makes me biscuits. Also, old men know that when the flash flood comes, to retreat to higher ground before it comes!"

He turned and mounted his horse. "We going to talk all day, or search for Deuce?" he asked as he began to trot out of camp.

Red jumped on his horse and shouted to Yellow Wing, "Come on girl! Grandfather is leaving right now"

CHAPTER 22

THE BEST LAID PLANS...

BEEN FINALLY ARRIVED at his apartment and searched all of the pockets on his backpack, then the console in his car. Once inside, he had ransacked all of the dresser drawers, then all of the kitchen cabinets. On a top shelf, above the coffee cups, sat a tray from a drive-up burger joint. As he pulled it down, the first smile of the day crossed his face. Sitting on a compact mirror, next to a straw, lay a small plasic coin bag half full of cocaine. Thirty minutes later, he was in his back yard firing up his gas BBQ grill. But there were no steaks or pork chops on the menu, not even burgers or hotdogs. Today's fare consisted only of flannel shirt and blue jeans, with a side order of tennis shoes, all sauteed in horse blood! In less than an hour, he had accomplished 2 of the 3 major items on his to do list. As he sat down with phone in hand, he began working on goal number 3.

"Trowbridge Forest Products, how may I direct your call?"

"Speak to Mr. Trowbridge, please."

"Whom may I say is calling?"

"Just tell him it's Ben."

"One moment, please."

"Well, hello Ben. I was wondering when I'd hear from you," answered the cultured southern drawl.

"Yes sir, I, uh, we found the uhh deeds and we had to uhh.."

"Wait a second Ben, slow down now. You say you did find the deeds? How many, and where are they?"

"I got them right here, sir!" Ben said in a rush. "There are 12 of them total and they encompass vast areas of acreage that are owned by you, or leased from the government by you!"

"Good job, son! Why don't you and Ronnie meet me at the Yacht Club tonight and I'll take a look at them. If they are as you say, then we'll discuss the other 10 grand I promised as a bonus. How about 10 p.m.?"

Ben's thoughts were bouncing around in his mind like a BB in a matchbox, trying to decide how to present the fact that he wanted much more than the 5 grand apiece after what they had went through! Should he tell Mr. Trowbridge what had happened? After all, he was saving him millions, so surely he could afford a hundred thousand each, right? With all of the different figures bouncing around in his head, he wasn't sure why he had settled on two hundred thousand, but once he did, everything came out in a rush.

"Well, Mr. Trowbridge, there has been a little change in plans. I'll be more than happy to meet you tonight, but instead of 10,000 dollars, we are going to 200,000. I know that is quite a bit more than our original deal, but you're going to save millions by destroying these deeds. And we had some serious complications to address after finding these deeds. Someone else found out that we had found them! That lawyer guy from Knoxville! The guy who originally found the site!"

"Wait, wait, what? You let somebody else see them?"

"No sir, no, we, uh, he, uh, well, he heard us talking after we had found them. And I sort of hit him! With a shovel! Twice! He was spying on us, and I didn't know what else to do!"

"Holy shit, son! Did you kill him? I know his Dad, and he is not someone you want for an enemy! Tell me you didn't kill him!"

"No, we didn't. I killed his horse. Then the horse fell on him. Then I butchered the horse up with bear claws and he was trapped under the horse and he was unconscious from the shovel blow and the bears are going to eat him and.."

"Dammit, son, slow down! Slow down a second!"

"Okay, okay, Mr Trowbridge! But you see why we need more money! And we did it for you!"

"Now Ben, I didn't tell you to kill anyone! But start from the beginning and tell me the whole story. And it will take me a day or so to get that much cash in small bills. I'm sure that's the way you'll want it, right? I'll have to draw it from an offshore account so that it won't show up on my company records. So, like I said, start from the beginning and go slow!"

As Ben began to tell his story again, Trowbridge reached over and hit the record button. He had purchased a phone with this feature several years ago and it had come in handy on many occasions.

Ronnie lie on his cot and tried to get a few minutes rest, but the drama of the night's events kept running through his mind like a cheap thriller. All he could think about, was what had they missed? Did he get all of the tracks erased well enough? Had the bears gotten to Deuce yet? Should he take a chance and go see? And if they had, should he be the one to find him? Everything had happened so quickly, and now what? He knew Ben had left with Dr. Trent, and had taken the deeds with him. Ben had also informed him of the change in payment plan. He had told him that he was going to try and get 50,000 dollars for each of them. Ronnie prayed that he would! With that much cash, he'd leave just as soon as he had the money in hand!

But right now, his main concern was Red and his grandfather. He had hoped that Red would be out of town, as usual. And the old man! He sure as hell hadn't seen that one coming! He had thought him to old and feeble to be out tracking anymore! The Search and Rescue guys were pretty good at tracking, but he considered himself just as good, if not better. But nobody compared to that old cantankerous bastard when it came to tracking! The old guy had told him once that he could track an individual fly across a field of cowpatties! Everyone had a good laugh at that, but as he had gotten to know him and his reputation over the years, he began to think that maybe he hadn't been joking!

In his earlier day, all of the Search and Rescue teams from the neighboring counties had used him at one time or another, as well as the Parks and Wildlife rangers. They had used him to track a bear that had developed a taste for horseflesh. By a single scar on the bear's right hind foot, he was able to distinguish it from all the other bears and track it to its' den! So, yeah, the old man showing up was worrisome!

Ronnie had just about dozed off when he heard a horse snort, then voices on a radio.

"Team 3 to base."

"Go ahead 3."

"Yeah, Rob, we found a set of tracks that look pretty recent. They seem to have the correct nail pattern that Red sent us. We are on a narrow game trail that skirts the edge of the canyon. In fact, you can see down into the canyon from here. The trail becomes too narrow for a horse, and we had to back out, then turn around on a ledge. There is no sign of them falling, but man, if they did, they wouldn't have survived!"

"Copy that, 3. Did you find any other tracks coming back down, over?"

"Well that's the funny thing about it. We have found some more tracks coming down, but they don't seem to be the same pattern. Hard to tell, what with all of the rocks and stuff. Maybe the old man should take a look, 10-4?"

"Copy that, 3. Mark it in red and if we don't find him soon, we'll get Red and the old man up there. Come on back down toward the canyon entrance and see if you can pick anything up from there, over."

"Rodger base. 3 out."

Ronnie breathed a sigh of relief. It seemed his trick on the southern trail was working. Now if only the same could be said for the north trail.

Which just happened to be where Red and Yellow Wing was walking their horses behind Grandfather. He had dismounted and dropped to his hands and knees. He was using his magnifying glass to study some tracks supposedly left by Ronnie that morning. But he had found something peculiar.

"Look at this, Red. We see Ronnie's tracks going east, and then over here, we see where he came back. But right here, there are too many tracks. Too many feet! Unless he has a 6 footed horse!"

When Red knelt to examine the tracks, he could see what the old man was talking about, 4 going up and 4 coming back, and 2 over to the left by themselves. They were off of the main trail and going up.

Grandfather looked at Red and said, "By some of the disturbances on the edge of the path, I think someone was trying to erase some of the tracks. Not a bad job, if you just glance at them quickly. But once you look closely, you can see the brush marks under Ronnie's tracks. And look, there is another partial track that has been stepped in by another horse."

Grandfather mounted his horse rather spryly for one his age, then took off at a trot. By the time thay had caught back up with him, he was once again on his hands and knees.

"Look!" he said as he pointed. "There are shoe prints on these leaves!"

He picked up two leaves and put them together side by side. Sure enough, there was a wavy pattern. The kind seen on numerous styles of tennis shoes. Deuce had taken to wearing moccasins again, so they weren't his. Yellow Wing had worked with Ronnie for many years and knew he wore cowboy styled boots. So who had been up here wearing tennis shoes?

As Grandfather examined the leaves with his magnifying glass, Yellow Wing could see the deep concern in his eyes and wrinkled brow.

"What is it, Grandfather? What do you see?" she asked, not liking that frown on Red's face either.

Red finally said what Grandfather had not wanted to.

"The only way to leave that kind of print, would be if the shoe were wet or muddy."

"But it hasn't rained in weeks!" said Yellow Wing, confused by Red's statement. Then she caught on, and quickly teared up. "It's blood, isn't it? Oh my God, it is blood on those leaves! Oh no, Red!"

"Hey, hey, just calm down girl! Yes, it's most likely blood, but that doesn't mean its Deuce's blood!

It could be animal blood that somebody stepped in. A hunter maybe."

Yellow Wing blinked back her tears. Grandfather, you can tell, can't you? You can, right? I mean if anyone can, it's you ...right?"

"Dear girl, if it was fresh blood and I could smell, rub or taste it, I might could tell. But day old blood on a leaf? Not even I am that good!"

He turned his back to her and once again started walking, studying the ground. After about a mile of silence, Grandfather turned to Red, "Use your radio to call for the medicine guy. Get him headed this way, just in case. I am seeing more tracks and more evidence where someone tried to erase them.

Whoever they were, they're pretty good, but got in too much of a hurry. I have now also seen boot heel impressions in the leaves on both sides of the trail, as well as the same bloody tennis shoe track. I have also positively identified Deuce's horse."

He looked at Yellow Wing. "Maybe you should stay here and wait on the medical guy. Red and I will go on around this bend. Red, maybe I should carry your pistol, too. You do have your 30.06 rifle with you, right?"

"No, Grandfather, I loaned it to Deuce, so it's either on his saddle or in his tent. But don't worry, I have my .308 with me. It's better for bear or hogs anyway. Here, take the pistol. The .40 cal. has a bit of a kick, but I'm sure you can handle it."

"Wait a second, you 2! You are not taking off and leaving me here! I go where you go!" Yellow Wing exclaimed.

The 2 men shrugged their shoulders and started walking carefully east. Grandfather stopped and put his finger to his lips.. "Shh, from here on out we must be quiet. Tie these horses to a tree."

He and Red had both seen the bear tracks intermingled with the leaves, as well as the occasional scat pile. More than one bear. They had also thought that maybe Yellow Wing shouldn't see what might lie ahead.

CHAPTER 23

FINDING DEUCE

WHEN DEUCE NEXT came to, he had hoped the pain might have resided some. No such luck. He lay perfectly still, as he realized what had awakened him. The grunting and snuffling sounds, even the slurping noises, were close, very close. It was still dark in the shadows of the cliff, but barely. The half moon was gone, and the morning sun was struggling to make its' presence known over the Appalachians. It was providing just enough light through the foliage and trees, just enough for Deuce to see several large boar starting to feast on the horse's neck. He knew they would next go for the eyes, genitalia, and under belly of the horse. All of the easiest access points, rather than try to tear through the thick hide. With their razor sharp tusks, he knew they could easily rip the horse wide open, but they were essentially lazy and would go the easy route first. That was about all that he knew about feral hogs. Well, that, and they would eat about anything, dead or alive! He wondered if maybe he should yell or try to make noises to scare them off? No, he'd better not. The way his damn luck was going, it'd just piss them off and make them attack him!

After that, he must have drifted off again, and when he came to this time, his olfactory senses were assaulted by a foul and pungent odor! Not 6 inches from his face was the ass end of a huge sow, steadily munching away on the face of his poor horse! Deuce came to tears as he thought about what they had done to the old mare. In his frustration, he drew back and struck the sow right below her tail, with all of the strength he could muster! With a surprised grunt and a squeal, she let out a fart the nearly gagged him, then headed for the brush! After he caught his breath, he began to laugh out loud, and the more he thought about it, the louder he laughed! The remaining hogs began to back away from the horse. All 4 of them were staring straight at him, and he was trying to imagine what they were thinking. And the more he thought, the more he laughed. Suddenly, the hogs turned and bolted for the dense brush behind them! He laughed some more, until his head was throbbing again. Then, in the sudden stillness, he heard a noise that made him wish the hogs would come back! A noise he hadn't heard since that TV special on Animal Planet. A special about black bears!

Deuce froze. He didn't know much more about bears, than he did about wild boar, but one thing he was pretty sure about; laughter and a smack on the ass wasn't going to work this time! He hoped being perfectly still was the right call! He had no choice anyhow, as he was scared stiff and couldn't move anything but his arms!

He knew they had to be looking for him by now, but he figured Ronnie and Ben would try to steer them away from this area as long as possible. Give the bears and hogs plenty of time to do their work. Seems like things were right on schedule for them! The bear was now circling the horse. It had undoubtedly detected the smell of man, and was being very cautious. But how long before hunger overrode caution? Were bears smarter than hogs? Deuce was trying to keep one eye partially open. He noticed the bear was getting closer with each orbit! Then the bear suddenly charged the horse, raking it with its' claws, then retreating! The claws had left deep gouges on its' rear flank, coming to within a foot of Deuce's body! It circled again, this time only a few feet away! Deuce figured it wouldn't be long now! And he was right! With a terrible ferocity that few ever see, and even fewer live to tell about, the bear attacked the hindquarter of the horse, ripping out huge chunks of hide and meat! Only a couple of feet away from Deuce's head, his terror strickenmind would not let him look! Even so, his ears relayed to his mind enough sound to make him visualize the carnage! And just as he screamed in terror, there was a loud BOOM! Bear blood and brains rained down all over him! He was still screaming and yelling at the bear when Red and Yellow Wing rushed up. Red was on his radio calling in all the help he could summon to try and get over 2000 pounds of dead animals off of his cousin! Grandfather had gone back after the horses, thinking they could use them to drag the bear and horse off of Deuce. Yellow Wing and Red both took off their jackets and began trying to wipe the blood and gore off of him. When Grandfather arrived with the water, they let him drink, then started cleaning him up again. The medic arrived and did a thorough check, informing everyone of the seriousness of Deuce's injuries, then blessed him with a large shot of morphine. It was the last thing he remembered until he woke up in the hospital with an Indian princess staring into his eyes!

CHAPTER 24

GUILT AND REDEMPTION

WHEN RONNIE HAD retired to his tent, he had kept the 2 way radio with him. Using the earplug insert, he had been able to quietly monitor the search teams. He had heard Yellow Wing's request for the medic, and had heard her admit that they hadn't yet found Deuce, but had found bloody footprints in the leaves and suspected the worse! The anxiety and stress in her voice was obvious, even over the radio. He knew it wouldn't be long now until they found Deuce.

Now Ronnie had a decision to make, and with his curiosity mingling with his fear and conscience, it was causing his thought process to spiral out of control. Coming up with a definitive plan of action seemed like a forlorn hope, at best. Then he heard the distant discharge of a large caliber rifle. Like maybe a .308 or 30.06 that Red was known to have had with him. Then the radio came alive with calls for help and the request for a helicopter! Red came on to explain to everyone that Deuce was still alive, though barely, and trapped under his horse and a bear that Red had shot! As he rattled off the co-ordinates for the chopper, Ronnie made his decision!

He rode into camp and headed straight for the supply tent. Fortunately, the camp was nearly deserted. The only people he saw were the S&R team member manning the radio, and Jonah White, from the university, who merely waved at him as he passed by. Once at the tent, he began to fill his backpack with non-perishable food items, extra batteries, matches, and anything else he thought might come in handy. He next visited the roped off section outside of the living area. This was where they kept the propane for the cookstoves and the gas for the 4 wheelers and generators. He filled up the 4 wheeler and strapped an extra 5 gallon can on the back rack. He then quietly idled his way back through the camp and headed due south.

His first objective was to reach a high point hoping his cell phone would then work. He had a cousin that he knew he could trust, and he needed him to go to his apartment and grab a few personal items, including his passport. The plan was to then meet him outside of Sylva in 2 days, and take him to the airport in Spartanburg, S. Carolina. There he could catch a plane to somewhere quick! At Sylva, he hoped to go to their little bank and cash a check for the monies in his savings and checking accounts. Then he would max out his credit cards before destroying them!

With all of this on his mind, thoughts of Ben and his part of the money were all but forgotten. And he honestly hoped Deuce would recover. His involvement in this debacle was the most shameful of atrocities he could ever imagine being a part of. What the hell had he been thinking?

Then he remembered the pictures he had taken with his cell phone. Pictures of all of the land deeds and the Union's promise to the Cherokee! If Ben did get the originals to Mr. Trowbridge, and he destroyed them, Ronnie still had proof of their existence! He could send them to Yellow Wing! Though it wouldn't exonerate him for his participation, it would help alleviate some of the guilt he felt.

With a plan of action now mapped out in his mind, Ronnie continued south on the winding trail, hoping to make it at least halfway before the trail quit or he ran out of gas.

He looked back at the Great Smoky Mountains, hoping to retain one final picture in his mind. One last vision of his home for 27 years.

Ben had worn a path in his carpet, pacing back and forth while waiting on Trowbridge's call. When he hadn't called by the second day, he began to get worried. His paranoia magnified by the cocaine, he began to envision all manner of things that could go wrong! And little did he know how right he was! At 3:30 that afternoon, the call finally came.

"Ben, my boy!"

"Yes sir, Mr. Trowbridge!"

"Just called to tell you that I finally have the money together. Can you meet me at the Yacht Club, down at my boat slip? We'll do this deal on my boat, where it's a bit more private. Say, about 9 p.m.?"

"Yes sir, yeah, okay. 9 p.m., right. No problem, slip number 72, right?"

"That's right, son, number 72. And bring Ronnie with you, too. I'd like to personally thank him for his help in this."

"Ah, well, I'm afraid that won't be possible at the moment, sir. He's still down at the dig site keeping an eye on things."

"I see. Well, that's okay, I guess. So, 9 p.m. sharp, Ben, and I'll still need to look at them, make sure they are what you sat they are. And, if so, then no problem. But I must warn you son, that I'll not be alone. There will be an associate of mine there. I'll not be sitting around alone with that kind of money. I'm sure you understand."

"Uh, well, yeah, though I'd prefer you be alone, I do see your point. 9 p.m. it is sir. See you then!"

"Right, Ben, see you then," Trowbridge said. He hung up the phone and turned to the 2 F.B.I. agents that had been listening in. The elder of the 2 nodded his head and said,

"Okay, sir. I'll be with you on the boat. Dennis here, and 2 other agents will be stationed out of sight, nearby. Do you think he will be armed?"

Trowbridge leaned back in his chair, took a drink of his scotch, thinking 'what an asinine question', then said, "I just imagine he will be. Anybody who would beat someone down with a shovel, and then kill and butcher a horse, is frankly quite capable of anything. And expecting to be carrying a quarter of a million dollars? Wouldn't you be armed?"

"Yes sir," replied the agent, "I sure as hell would be."

CHAPTER 25

BEN GETS HIS

RED AND GRANDFATHER watched the helicopter lift off with both Deuce and Yellow Wing aboard. After several members of the Search and Rescue team had arrived, they had used their horses and manpower to extricate Deuce from beneath the animals. Due to the morphine, he had been blissfully unaware of the procedure, even of the mile or so trip to where the chopper had found a place to land. The EMT who had examined Deuce now turned and gave them his rough diagnosis.

"It's not good, Red. Two severe lacerations on his skull, a definite concussion, maybe even a fracture of the cranium in an area called the parietal bone. The swelling and pressure could have caused serious trauma to the brain. Only a specialist can tell you more on that. While that's bad enough, both of his legs sustained injuries when the horse fell on him. The lower leg bone, or tibia, of the left leg is definitely broken, and right femur, or thighbone, seemed to be disjointed where it meets the hip trochanter or acetabulum, uh, the concave area where the femur attaches to the pelvic bone. But, man, there is just something not right about how he landed in that position. He would have nearly had to be laying down on his back and just let the horse fall on him!"

Red too, had been wondering how Deuce had come to be in that position. And what had made the horse fall in the first place?

Apparently, Grandfather had also been pondering the same mystery, for when Red turned around to speak with him, he was over at the horse's body. His arms were buried up to his elbows, deep inside the poor mare's chest cavity.

He suddenly exclaimed, "Aha! Got it!"

He then stood up and began to wipe his arms and hands off on Red's already blood soaked jacket.

"What is it, Grandfather? What did you find?"

"It could have been possible that the hogs, or maybe the bear, startled the mare and she reared up, causing Deuce to be thrown and her to fall. But it wouldn't have killed her. And as bad as the carnage looks, it wasn't the hogs or bear that killed her. Not unless they have now learned how to use guns, and if that's the case, we are in serious trouble! In her chest, I found this."

He then threw a mushroom shaped lead ball to Red.

"It can only be from a large caliber pistol. Like maybe Deuce's .357? Where is it, by the way? It wasn't on him."

"It's not in his saddle bags, either. I looked when we stripped all of the gear off of the horse," replied Red.

The old man stared off at the horizon, and began to speak in a strong voice that made him seem decades younger. "Here is what I think happened. According to the tracks we discovered coming up here, 2 people either brought or followed Deuce here. Once here, Deuce was hit on the head with something, by someone. They took his pistol and positioned the horse over him or beside him. Someone who knows the anatomy of a horse, for most people do not know precisely where the heart is. They then shot the horse directly in the heart, killing her instantly, causing her to fall to her side and land on his legs and waist. Then they cut her around the entrance wound in hopes that the hogs and bears would start there. I don't know why someone didn't hear the gunshot, but we were lucky the hogs hadn't dug to far yet, or they might have ingested the bullet! Some of these claw marks don't fit either. Look at how deep the gouges are at the rear flank, where we saw the bear attack. These others were done by something much weaker. More like a man would do!"

Red scratched his head and looked at the old man. The hard look on his face reminded Red of why Grandfather was so respected, if not downright feared by some.

"But who would do such a thing? And why?" asked Red of his grandfather.

Grandfather looked him straight in the eyes and said, "I am pretty sure who, but have no idea why."

Then in a raspy tear-choked voice, he said, "Come along, Red, let us go have a chat with one Mr. Cloud, and ask him why he chose to hurt my grandson. And, his buddy Ben, too. We need to visit with him, also!"

As they walked toward their horses, Grandfather asked him a question that sent chills down his spine.

"You have plenty of rope? And matches? Plenty of matches? We may need them to find out the why part!"

◆◆◆◆◆

At about 20 minutes before 8, Ben put Ronnie's pistol in the right pocket of his jacket and placed the deeds in his briefcase. He had spread them out and placed them between clear plastic photo album sheets so that they were easily legible. 45 minutes later, he was approaching the Yacht Club from the north. His mouth was so dry he could barely swallow. So instead of going to the boat slip early, he decided to see if they would let him into the lower bar for a drink or 2. He had plenty of time. His earlier sense of urgency was now being fueled by his paranoia, but he needed a few drinks to calm himself.

The bartender must have recognized him from before, and didn't bother asking him for a membership card, or even a guest card. Didn't even look at him funny when he ordered 2 double Beam's and coke, downed them in a few swallows, and ordered 2 more. At 20 dollars each for a double, he had just spent 80 bucks in 15 minutes, but tonight it was worth it! By the time he was on his fourth drink, the mellow buzz of the Jim Beam was starting to relax him some. He was just sitting idly and looking out at all of the beautiful boats in their berths, when something strange caught his eye. A sudden movement at about slip number 68.

Suddenly, a man in a suit stepped out onto the walkway. As he did so, another guy in a suit stepped out from the boat slip across from him. They stood there and talked a minute, then Ben saw one of them reach up and speak into his coat sleeve! Then guy number 2 did the same thing! Radio check! Mike test, Ben's paranoid brain screamed! How many times had he seen that very thing on TV?

Just as he sat his drink down, the first guy started talking into his sleeve again, and was staring straight at him! Ben had seen enough! Enough to know something wasn't right! His bullshit alarm was screaming at maximum volume, and all he could think about, was get to the car! He grabbed his briefcase and ran up the stairs to the parking lot. He wasn't thinking law enforcement. He was thinking that Trowbridge had hired someone to take the deeds away, and maybe even kill him! He ran at breakneck speed across the parking lot, jumped in his car, so glad he hadn't locked it!

He backed out and slammed it into Drive, just as one of the suits ran out in front of him, gun drawn, and yelled "F.B.I. Stop where you are..." is about all that Ben heard, then a series of thumps and bumps as he ran into him! F.B.I.? Yeah, bullshit, thought Ben! As he sped toward the exit, he spotted the second suit running over to help his buddy. That ought to keep them busy for awhile, he thought, and just as looked straight again, 2 black Ford LTD's were pulling in to block the exit! He spun the steering wheel left, hoping to go around them through the grass. He didn't notice the 8 foot wide, 10 foot deep drainage ditch, at least not until he hit the concrete retainer wall!

The only thing that had kept him from going through the windshield had been the car's airbag! He popped the door open and just sat there, stunned! Just as ammonia can be used to arouse the senses, the smell of the gas now leaking from his car had the same effect on Ben! He exited the car, falling six feet to the bottom of the concrete ditch. He was just getting to his feet, when several men with guns began to yell commands at him.

"Put your hands up!"

"Put your hands behind you!"

"Climb up here, do it now!"

"Lay down in the ditch!"

"Freeze, don't move!"

They were all yelling something different! Ben was so disoriented and confused that he just let his animal instincts take over; he ran! And good thing he did! He hadn't gone 20 feet when someone yelled, "Fire! Fire!" Ben just knew it was a verb and not a noun he was hearing! Then there was a tremendous KAW-WOOMPH! and Ben was thrown into the air! Right before he landed in the ditch, he wondered, "What the hell did they shoot me with?" Then the lights went out…

--------- ✦✦✦✦✦ ---------

Agent Steen was the only one hurt by the explosion, but not too bad. He looked more like the victim of a barbecue gone bad than a car explosion. Agent Lloyd, on the other hand, hadn't fared to well in his attempt to stop a moving car. He had suffered a broken leg and several broken ribs. When the fire was put out and the massive wrecker had lifted the car from out of the ditch, the F.B.I. executed a search warrant for the now wet and charcoal interior of the car. Not much was found of the briefcase, just a couple of hinges, and what might be the locking mechanism. If there had been any historical documents, they were now part of an ash and melted plastic glob! Trowbridge couldn't believe his luck! Not only did he get immunity for his part and co-operation, he also saved 200,000 dollars, and the deeds were destroyed anyway!

Ben was in custody, and the F.B.I. were on their way to apprehend Ronnie Cloud. With the taped conversations Trowbridge had provided the F.B.I., it was more than enough for an arrest warrant, as well as search warrants for both of their apartments. But the F.B.I. soon discovered they weren't the only one's looking for Mr. Cloud! The Tribal Police and the Search and Rescue teams had been combing the reservation and surrounding forests for him, also.

At the end of the second day, Red and Grandfather had located the 4 wheeler, then tracked Ronnie for several miles on foot. When they came to a narrow paved road, they lost all sign of him. Red concluded that someone in a car must have picked him up. The F.B.I. raided his apartment and found no indication or clues as to where he might have gone. When they tried to put a freeze on his checking and savings accounts, they discovered they were both empty. When they tried to track his credit cards usage, they were informed by both Visa and Mastercard that he had maxed out their cards by way of emergency cash draws at a branch of his home bank in Sylva, N.C. He was gone, adios, adieu, auf wiedersehen, sayanora, and see ya! His name and photo were immediately sent out to all F.B.I. offices and state and local authorities.

--------- ✦✦✦✦✦ ---------

EPILOGUE

October, 2007

Deuce finished his breakfast of oatmeal and toast, all the while wishing for biscuits and gravy, sausage and eggs, deer steak and home fries, and coffee, real coffee, Grandfather's coffee! Not this watered down crap. Why, you could see the bottom of the cup, even when it was full! If I could just walk a little better, I'd be up and out of here pronto, he thought. He went to jump up, as if he could really do it, by God! Then the dizziness and nausea assaulted him, causing him to lie back down quickly. Dumbass, he thought to himself as he reached for the remote. He looked at the clock and smiled, eight a.m. on a Tuesday morning. Yellow Wing would be here in another hour, and along with her this time would be Red and Grandfather. Maybe Grandfather. He hadn't been off of the reservation but once or twice in the last 10 years. But, Red had promised that the old man would come, even if he and Yellow Wing had to hogtie and carry him! Deuce had noticed that Red was sure to include her in that statement, for she stood a much better chance of persuading him than he did!

The F.B.I. had come by several times to confirm different parts of the story. Convenient for them, too, having an agent laid up right down the hall! And their part of the story was nearly as interesting as his!

Deuce was just dozing off again, when he thought he felt a presence near him. He opened his eyes to find a wrinkled leather face staring at him with amused brown eyes.

"Wake Up! I didn't come all of this way to watch you sleep! I have seen that many times before, quite boring. I come to hear your whole story. Even

137

the part about how you let some city fellow sneak up and hit you with a shovel! Twice! I have told everyone that they were mistaken! Now I need to hear your version so we can make up a better story!"

"But, Grandfather, that would be lying!"

"So? Better to lie to people than to have them believe that I hadn't taught you better!" Red and Yellow Wing entered the room carrying extra chairs.

"Now cousin," Red started, "I want to hear the complete story, from the moment you had your first suspicions until the second I shot the bear! And by the way, you're welcome for that. Best 100 yard shot I ever made!"

"Grandfather said it was more like 40 yards."

"Yeah? Well he's old and can't see shi...uh ...very far!"

Deuce had just finished telling his story from front to back. The only part he had left out, was when the bear had attacked the horse's flank and he had wet himself...

The doctor had run everybody out while he poked and prodded, asking stupid questions, like, does that hurt? Hell yes it does! When he was through, the nurse added some more pain killer to his I.V. drip, and he got all warm and fuzzy.

The next time he woke up, Yellow Wing was sitting next to his bed. She had been there nearly every time he had opened his eyes. Right now, his biggest fear wasn't the inevitable limp he was going to have, or not even the possible brain damage he may have incurred from the head injury. No, his primary fear was waking up and her no longer being there!

While he could orate and litigate with the best of them, it seemed he always had trouble speaking around her. Now, after several botched attempts, he had managed to convey his message. She had squeezed his hand and kissed his brow, promising to be there forever.

And she had meant it. Together they were going to write a book about the legend of the Cherokee maps, and maybe next time when he woke up, she would show him the pictures Ronnie Cloud had sent her...maybe..

The End

For now ....

Printed in the United States
By Bookmasters